CITY OF
LIGHT

About Rebecca Laffar-Smith

Born to the magical beauty of her sunburnt country home in Western Australia, Rebecca Laffar-Smith always yearned to explore the wonders of this world and beyond. After twelve years as a freelance writer and editor, she gave up writing about the non-fiction world in favour of the fantastical creatures and fanciful things she could create and immortalise in fiction. Now she writes in the moments she can steal away from home-schooling her son and daughter, and volunteering as an events coordinator and mentor for her local writing community. She dreams of someday running a farm-stay writer's retreat on the outskirts of Perth and writing her stories in a detached, hexagonal room with floor to ceiling bookshelves and plenty of natural light.

http://www.rebeccalaffarsmith.com

CITY OF LIGHT

REBECCA LAFFAR-SMITH

City of Light

First published in Australia in 2018 by Rebecca Laffar-Smith

National Library of Australia Cataloguing-in-Publication entry:
Author: Laffar-Smith, Rebecca, author.
Title: City of Light / Rebecca Laffar-Smith
ISBN: 978-0-6482286-3-9 (Paperback)
            978-0-6482286-8-4 (eBook)

Cover design by The Cover Collective

To the Smarter Artists
and the Novel Nights Crew

For the inspiration,
and unerring support.

1

Woken by a Blue Giant

Niah

It feels strange to wake up for the first time.

A shrill piercing shriek echoes through me. It reverberates through frame after frame, bouncing around me as if ricocheting down long arched corridors. The sound bounces through every vessel in my body.

My skin tingles as my nerve endings awaken. The solid weight of the bed beneath me sits on my skin, or perhaps I sit on it, or did I lie? It stretches out beneath me, under my feet, my hips, my thighs, my back, my shoulders, my neck, my head. Solid, and really there rather than just in my imagination or my dreams.

I open my eyes and blink, blinded for a moment before focusing. Red lights flash in epic fury around me. They create a melodramatic air of dark menace over every surface. The thick, heavy panels of white, chrome, and light-emitting diode screens in green, white, and black fill the walls and ceiling in front of my eyes but even they seem to turn a mottled blood red with each blink.

My heart, thudding rapidly, stutters as I realise something is very, very wrong.

"MALFUNCTION! MALFUNCTION!" A disembodied female voice echoes from the walls over the wailing of the alarm.

A white blur speeds past the corner of my eye and I sit up to catch sight of it before it disappears around the curve of the corridor at the end of the room.

"MALFUNCTION!" It echoes, its own voice pitched lower, like a masculine counterpart to the feminine pitch of the emergency alert.

I feel my head spin and wonder when I last ate or drank. My body feels strangely saturated as if it has been strung out for weeks. My mouth, dry and heavy as if I'd not used it in hundreds of orbits.

As I push myself to my feet, I see another flash of white speed past the door. "Wait!" I cry out. As it whizzes by, it seems to draw to a halt then back up without turning around. I see it better then, a bobble head on a strangely conic shaped geometrically perfect body. The white must be a kind of metal. It gleams in curves. As it reaches the door, the strange head rotates in place first, and then the body swivels to match it. Twin pale blue orbs of light peer out of a black screen like eyes gazing at me.

We stare at each other like that for a moment. Around us, the red lights flash and the siren blares. The noise still thrums through me and I feel its urgency.

When it seems like the being before me will not speak I say, "Is something the matter?"

On its dark face, a strip of light forms above its 'eye' and lifts, as if the machine is raising an eyebrow. "Malfunction?" it says in its low robotic voice.

I blink. "I am?"

It tips its bobble head slightly then lifts its body casement. "Sleeper. We have not arrived. You should be sleeping."

"But I'm awake."

"Yes." It pauses as if considering this. A scroll of strange symbols replaces its eyes as hundreds of words race down its screen and then disappear. The eyes blink open from slits, blink again, then gaze out at me. "Malfunction."

"Can I help?"

"Hybrid clone one, strand November-One-Alpha-Four is awake. Elixr, run diagnostic on clone sleeping unit."

The feminine emergency alert voice responds. "Error, diagnostics not available. Processor overload. Malfunction."

The robot blinks again, its strange eyes oddly expressive as it shows confusion. "Malfunction! Yes." Suddenly, it turns, head first and then body, and whizzes off out the door and down the corridor again.

I glance around but there is nothing in the room that might shed some light on what is going on so I walk out into the corridor and follow the glowing trail of blue-green light that seems to linger in the wake of the strange droid.

The ship around me echoes its theme of white and chrome down the corridor. Open portals pocket the walkway but the rooms inside are bare and empty. Most have a single raised platform like the bed I only recently vacated. But as I follow the fading threads of the trailing light, I come into a much larger room.

The view from floor-to-ceiling windows stills my breath. Beyond it glows a small orb of sparkling blue-purple surrounded by a vast blanket of black. A shiver runs over me as I realise the orb is growing incrementally bigger in the heartbeats between my first seeing it and the next flashing alert. A screen suspended from the ceiling flashes words, symbols, markers, and shapes as if the same alert flashed past in a rapidly alternating script of foreign languages. I recognise the words, at least some of the time, COLLISION ALERT.

"It's not even that close. Can't we just steer around?" I shout over the sound of the alarm.

The robot turns its head as if just noticing me. "November-One-Alpha-Four, you must return to sleep. It is not time."

"But there's an emergency. Maybe I can help."

"There is a malfunction. Elixr and I will have it in hand shortly."

I'm not sure I can believe that. It certainly doesn't seem like anyone is doing much of anything, and I don't see any crew members around to help.

"Elixr, reacquire and assign navigation controls immediately."

The eerie female voice comes through the walls again. "Error, navigation not available. Processor overload. Malfunction."

"Yes, you warped hunk of metal space scrap. Processor overload. Do you ever say anything else?"

"I apologise if my recent interactions have expressed vocabulary lacking in diversity, Harttade. What is it you would have me say?"

"Say you've fixed it! Get us back online!"

There is a quiet moment as if she is processing her confusion. "I am unable to comply as my voice avatar ship-wide communication and support services unit is not equipped with a fabrication drive. The malfunction is not repaired. The processor is overloaded. We are not online."

"Stupid bucket of bolts." The droid spins away from one screen and begins tinkering with another.

I frown. "Why is the processor overloaded?" Neither voice responds to me so I say it again. "Someone, tell me why the processor is overloaded."

The female voice responds. "Seven of sixteen processor drives are offline. Remaining systems have reached processing capacity in the random access memory. Main systems online are ship-wide life-support, clone sleeping bays four, seven, and eleven through nineteen, proximity alert sensors, warp-activation, sublight propulsion engines..." She continues listing other key systems before finishing with, "and Elixr voice-avatar, ship-wide communication and support services."

"Can we shut down non-essential systems?"

A moment passes as the question is processed. "Ship commands recognise November-One-Alpha-

Four command. Shutting down non-essential systems." The alarm falls silent and the flashing red lights cease. I blink, finding their absence almost deafening after the noise.

The robot head spins toward me again. "What did you do?"

I shrug. "Apparently, I shut down non-essential systems."

"Elixr, reclaim navigation controls."

"Please wait, still processing vitality statistics of previous command."

"What? How long will that take?"

"Please wait, unable to compute duration of processing procedure until processing of vitality statistics in previous command are complete."

"Daft bolt-trap." His head swivels to the window and his strange lit eyes widen, then blink. I turn and see what had previously been a distant star looming larger and larger. Spouts of liquid fire jettison from the blue giant's surface. I gasp, stepping back as the flame reaches out to engulf us. It hisses over a sheen of green energy that arcs to life around us a few hundred feet from the glass. "Elixr, override previous command, reinstate navigation controls immediately."

The shield glows, fending back the streaming flames. "Authorisation verified. Navigation transferred to hybrid autonomous research, telemetry, teleportation, and defence engine one."

The droid's strange, robotic hands rise. As if guiding a giant ocean liner, he begins spinning an invisible wheel. In the window, the orb appears to suddenly veer to the right as the ship comes about and pulls away from the star's gravity well. Once clear of the jet-stream from the blue giant's solar flare, the green haze of the ship's shield fades to clear. "Elixr, replot course."

"Error. Processing capacity still at maximum levels. Unable to process request. Malfunction."

The droid blinks. "But the alarms stopped. It's fixed."

"Incorrect. The alarms are a non-essential system and were desisted in previous command. Would you like to reinstate?"

"Negative, Elixr. Activating stop function to effect repairs."

I stumble forward as the ship comes to a rapid halt. Beside me, the droid remains suspended in place and so ends up several feet behind me. I turn. "Why did we feel that?" I ask the droid. He ignores me.

The voice from the walls responds. "Inertial dampening reduced to twenty-percent efficiency as computed by vitality statistics."

"And now we're standing still in the void of space?"

"Affirmative." The voice pauses a moment then resumes. "Accuracy adjustment. Negative. Elixr is suspended in a non-propulsion state in Azure Sector Seventy-Six-Fifty near the apex point of a spiral nebula in the Asper System. Seven hundred and fourteen light cycles and eleven point five nine light ticks from Nar."

"Replot course!" The robot shouts.

"Error. Processing capacity still at maximum levels. Unable to process request. Malfunction."

"But you just stated our exact position."

"Current plot point is a necessary function of navigation and maintained to exact star-map coordinates in processor twelve."

I glance at the robot. "If I understand correctly, the biggest malfunction is that there are several processors offline?"

He looks at me as if he's factoring in my priority in the list of emergencies he is currently dealing with. Eventually, his blue-lit eyes blink and a line of blue lights up beneath his eyes and curves in a makeshift smile. He extends a hand toward me.

"Greetings, November-One-Alpha-Four. I am Harttade, a Hybrid Autonomous Research, Telemetry, Teleportation, and Defence Engine. You are aboard the Elixr. She is a masterful state-of-the-art interstellar research vessel that departed Nar almost two hundred narcycles ago. You were created following BLEEP to complete our mission."

"Bleep?"

His head tilts. "Oh, forgive me. It appears aspects of my historical records are unable to be accessed at this time."

"What do you mean I was created?"

"Your genetic material was constructed from DNA in our archives. Your body remained in a hibernation sleep for sixteen narcycles, three orbits, two circuits, fifteen factors, twenty-three deccas, and sixteen ticks."

"I was asleep?"

"Affirmative. Your consciousness was unnecessary to operations as we traversed star systems on our return to Nar."

"Unnecessary…" I swallow as I consider my life, sixteen narcycles of it, had been denied me because I was deemed unnecessary. I wish I could control the wash of tears from my eyes. I scrub them away with the back of my hand and bite my lip.

Hart blinks. "Your emotional response is not computable."

"I've been asleep for sixteen narcycles! Forgive me if it takes a few deccas to get used to the idea that my whole life is a fabrication and that I wasn't deemed worthy enough to wake up."

"You and Whisky-One-Sierra-Four were to be revived once we reach our destination."

"What is Whisky-One-Sierra-Four?"

He waves a hand at the screen above us and an image blinks into place. "Whisky-One-Sierra-Four." On the screen, in another blank room, is a sleeping platform. On it, another girl sleeps. Her long, blonde hair lies in straight rows beside her pale face. Her body is wrapped like mine in the slim lines of a full-body skin-tight suit of grey and white.

"She's a Narian."

"Yes, her genetic material was constructed from DNA in our archives."

"Wake her up."

"Negative, her consciousness is not necessary to operations."

I spin, marching down the hall. "Take me to her. I want to see her."

Hart hovers behind me a moment and then trails me down the hall. "Her consciousness is not necessary to operations."

15

"You don't just leave someone alone for their whole life."

"She is asleep."

"She is alive!" I stop, and gaze up at the walls and ceiling around me. "Computer, show me the way."

A yellow light flickers on the wall and a trail of panels flash in one direction. "Greetings November-One-Alpha-Four. I am Elixr. At your command."

I blink. "At my command?"

"Indeed."

Interesting. But first things first. "Lead us to the girl."

I follow the trail of yellow lights down a long corridor. As I pass them, they blink out and the corridor behind us falls into darkness. Nothing but the faint trace of azure haze from Hart's trail lingers. Eventually we arrive at an alcove and there she is. I step close to the bed and run my fingers down her hair. Against her collarbone, I notice a metal tag on her sleeper suit that reads. 'W.1.S.4.'

"Wish?"

Hart hovers beside me. "Whisky-One-Sierra-Four."

"Elixr, wake her up."

"Processing request."

Moments later, the girl sighs. I stroke my fingers down her arm as she blinks her eyes open. "Hey there. How are you?"

She gazes up at me, her ice-blue eyes full of sleepy shadows. She blinks at me, swallows, then licks her lips. "What–" She stops, then shakes her head.

16

"You've been asleep a long time. And, if you're anything like me, you're both hungry and thirsty."

She nods and pushes herself upright. "I'm starving."

I turn to Hart. "Food and drink?"

"You should both return to sleep. Your nutritional needs are met by the clone support systems when you are in stasis."

"But we're not sleeping, we're living. And living things need to eat."

A blue line pops up beneath his eyes as a mouth of sorts forms a clear arch of displeasure. "You are not necessary to operations."

"The ship is broken. Maybe we can help fix it."

Elixr's voice comes online. "November-One-Alpha-Four contains genetic memory ideally suited to factoring in my repairs."

Wish taps the silver circle of metal on my suit. "Niah."

I glance down but can't see the tag. "Niah?"

She smiles at me. "Niah."

"And Wish." I grin, tapping her own disk.

Hart hums and I wonder if it's some sort of bluster of discontent. "If you've both quite finished. We need to get up and running as soon as possible."

"Food and drink first. The ship's not going anywhere. And we've slept long enough that I should be able to work through the night as soon as we've eaten."

"Negative," Elixr says, "Nar-time is currently factor seven past midnight."

"Factor seven?" I ask.

"Nar time," Hart replies. "It's early morning on Nar."

"Well then, breakfast first and we can work all day."

He makes an odd noise as if releasing a huff of air. "Fine. But don't expect fine dining. The fabricator is offline so you'll be subjected to ration bars and spirit water."

"Sounds like heaven to me." I wink at him and a spark of blue lights up above his eye as he raises an eyebrow. "Lead on."

2

Genetic Skillsets

Niah

The morning break room is a relaxed space with teak flooring, soft light, and an inviting spirit of communal living. Wish and I take seats across from each other in two of the comfortable leather chairs. A cluster of four chairs is set around each of the three small tables in the room. Hart flashes off to one side of the room where he collects an assortment of packages and tubes from what looks like a long filing cabinet. "Ration bars and spirit water. These are designed to keep for millennia and are stored for emergencies." He drops his takings on the table between us. Wish snatches up the first packet, tearing into it with vigour and chomping down without really looking at the strange mash of ingredients.

I pick up a bar, opening it more carefully and examining the mix of oat-like flakes and fruit-like nuggets. It feels strangely familiar although, somehow, I know I've never actually eaten one before. My mouth and stomach react as if they already know I'll enjoy it. The mix of knowing blended with the lack of memories is disconcerting, so I bite cautiously. I'm instantly rewarded by a familiar taste that feels enhanced a thousandfold. My taste buds light up and I munch the rest of the bar swiftly, then delve around in the packets to try a few of the other assorted flavours.

The tubes of spirit water are another oddity. The chrome cylinders are secure and waterproof and the liquid inside has a thick, glutinous consistency more like sloppy jelly than water. But it's refreshing, chilled, and tastes sweetly fresh as if drawn from crisp, icy springs.

As Wish and I eat, Hart hovers impatiently and sighs. Sensing his frustration I turn to him between mouthfuls and ask, "What can you tell us about the problems with the ship?"

"There is a malfunction."

"I understand that, but what is the nature of it?"

He sighs. "You would not understand."

I raise an eyebrow. "You said I was created to complete a mission? Surely I've got some uses. You did intend to wake me up at some point, right?"

He hovers another moment and then sighs heavily before crossing to 'sit' in one of the two remaining chairs. Sit, is an odd way to consider his posture given that he has no legs as such to sit with. His body hovers above the chair, and tilts as if at rest, but is still at least two inches from the leather surface. A trail of blue from what must be hover jets seems to pool beneath him. Once settled, he continues. "Your role only becomes fundamental once we have returned to Nar."

"But surely a ship this size needs a crew."

He tilts his head. "A crew is normally stipulated and we had one. But fundamentally a crew is unnecessary. Elixr is pre-programmed to maintain systems and I am designed to control navigation and defence."

Wish leans forward. "What happened to your crew?"

Hart glances between the two of us. I wonder if he's attempting a fabrication or considering ignoring her question. Eventually he responds. "There was an incident."

It looks like Hart is about to explain but then a rapid scroll of text floods across his face. He emits a series of high pitched screeches. Wish and I lift our hands to protect our ears from the noise. Moments later, Hart's face clears. His eye orbs blink open and he continues as if nothing happened.

"The crew is unnecessary. Elixr and I can ensure we reach our destination."

"Unless something goes wrong. Something's wrong with you, isn't it?"

He huffs as if frustrated. I'm not sure if he's judging his own sense of failure or if my questions are bothersome.

"I really would like to help, Hart. How would a crew manage the problems you're facing?"

He pauses a long moment, considering my question, and I wonder if he will tell me or if he'll send us back to the sleeper bays instead.

"Hart?"

"Captain Bellamy would uncover the root of any

system failures from the research lab main computer. Maintenance members would fabricate and repair damaged hardware while my Captain dynamically updated internal systems and repaired any corruptions that may have occurred to the data."

"Can't you and Elixr just fix yourselves?" Wish asks.

"We do not have the same functional knowledge of our base code or interiors. Elixr manages the circuit-to-circuit functioning as a whole but not the underlying programming that creates her network of systems."

I nod, understanding without really understanding how I know what he's talking about. "And there are faults in the underlying programming?"

"Invariably, to some degree."

"So you need someone to run through lines of code."

"Fundamentally."

"Can't you do that?" Wish asks. She's working on what might be her sixth ration bar but has finally started to slow down.

"I am a research, telemetry, teleportation, and defence unit. Understanding of interstellar computational base code is not in my core memory deposits."

I sigh. "So, that's a no. Can I help you?"

His eyes flash as if sparked by an idea. "You are November-One-Alpha-Four, with the genetic memory of your primary DNA components."

"Um, I thought we established that my name is

Niah."

He tilts his head, then nods once. "Niah, you have the automatic nerve memories of your genetic material."

"And she was a programmer?"

The dots of his blue eyes blink. "He was our captain."

I let the new information land, but find myself drawn to deal with one particular point rather than the eagrim's nest of the rest of it. "He? But I'm a girl."

"There was a malfunction prior to the initiation of your cloning sequence."

I bite my lip because I suddenly realise my whole life might be a mistake. "What do you mean?"

"Elixr and I were forced to implement some augmentations to your DNA structure during the cloning sequence. We no longer had an original source of genetic material and the resource we used to fabricate your genetic structure was," he pauses, searching for the word, "damaged."

"Damaged? How?"

"Significant data corruption occurred during the BLEEP. Oh! Excuse me." He lifts his hand to the screen where I imagine his mouth might be if he had more than flashing lights for a face. The dots of his eyes disappear behind a screen of text again. I catch the words "data recovery" and "systems memory repair mode" between his fingers but most of it scrolls past before I can fully understand it. His eyes blink back into place and the text disappears. "It appears aspects of my historical records are unable to be accessed at this time."

I grimace. "Malfunction?"

"The damage to our systems is," he pauses, "extensive."

Wish leans forward. "But Niah can help you fix it right? If she's a clone of the captain?"

The rapid nod of Hart's head is disconcerting in speed and intensity. He rises up over the chair, then darts across the room, turns, and darts back. "Yes, yes! Come!"

"But–" I reach for a final sip and feel him practically bobbing with excitement beside me.

"Come, Niah. Come!"

I grab another unopened tube of spirit water as I push myself to my feet. Wish stands beside me as Hart darts back to the door. He zips out into the corridor, so I follow the trail of his blue stream. I glance back to see Wish gather up a stash of the rations and cylinders. If the slim-line body suit she wears had pockets, I imagine she'd be stashing everything within them. Instead, she settles for as much as she can carry. I shake my head. "It's not like anyone is going to steal it while we're gone. There's no one else around."

She shrugs. "When you feel like you've never eaten in your life, it's easy to worry you might never eat again." I swallow and nod because I know exactly where she's coming from. I'm already terrified of falling asleep in case I never wake up.

"Come on, before we lose Hart for good."

She tilts her head. "Not sure that's entirely a bad thing." She winks at me. "I'm itching to explore without a chaperon."

"We have time. But first, let's go see about the

programming. Maybe you can help."

She shrugs. "I've got no idea what you two were talking about."

"Want to check it out anyway?"

She nods. "Let's go!"

We have to jog down the corridor to catch up with the disappearing strands of Hart's hover stream as they turn a corner. The small bot comes about in front of a pair of heavy doors. "Come on, come on!" As we reach him, he hums and the doors open with a ping. He steps inside the small cylindrical chamber and turns to face us. He waves us in with his hands. "Come on!"

We both step inside and the doors swoosh closed behind us. The strange sensation of vertical movement tingles through me as we rapidly ascend. The doors swoosh open again on a new and unfamiliar corridor. Above us, a row of circular light panels blink on in rapid succession down the long channel. The walls are plain, smooth, white and featureless. This corridor is much narrower than any of the others we moved through downstairs. The final light illuminates a large door in the distance. It has the words "Research Lab" blazed across it in giant orange letters.

Hart whizzes off down the corridor and almost slams into the door as it fails to open. He rears back, a strange motion of backwards hovering over his own jet stream. He approaches the door again more slowly but it still does not open, so he glances around. "Elixr, activate door controls to the research lab."

A moment of silence passes, then Elixr's voice comes through the walls. "Negative. Unable to process your request."

I step forward, pull open the panel on the wall beside the door, and navigate the menu. It is second nature to me. Beside me, I feel Hart and Wish lean close as they curiously peer around me at the screen. After a few more clicks, the door slides open and the room beyond flickers into a wash of base-lit glass screens. Wide, white fibreglass desks cradle the room in a fractured oval. They ring a large round platform. Above each of the desks are large holo-screens trailing symbols and images similar to those creating light in the giant glass panels that surround the room.

"Wow!" Wish says beside me. My face mirrors hers. Although familiar in that eerie sense that everything seems to be familiar, this room is mind-blowing – beautiful even. I feel a tingle of excitement and my fingers itch to explore the high tech consoles. The screens flash with an array of information. My gaze wanders the room as I try to decide where to put my attention.

Hart crosses into the room and directly to a podium against the far wall, or is it a window? It's hard to tell because of the way the screen lights up in the glass. The surfaces are opaque so we can't actually see through them like the glass on the bridge, but they have similar floor to ceiling size. Hart turns when he reaches the podium and waves me forward again.

"You must fix the processors and regain full function of the ship. Come on."

I cross the room and join him at the podium. Its touch screen is a highly detailed input terminal. As I begin to explore the settings, instinctively familiar with the system's complexities, I glance up at the large holo display before me. Information scrolls into place and my hands move across the terminal in confident motions. I almost forget Hart and Wish are beside me as I delve into the intricate coding of the machine. Hart's soft hum – I'm not sure if it's contentment or impatience – is like a quiet bee in my ear, and the food packets crinkle in Wish's arms as she shifts on her feet. Knowing both are waiting, I focus on the primary objective; identifying the source of malfunction. My fingers fly across the screen until I find the relevant programs. I follow each twist in the ornate programming then sigh. Eventually, I tap an interface on the screen that puts the system into a diagnostics mode and turn to Hart and Wish.

"Well, have you fixed it?"

"I'm afraid it's not that simple. This will take several factors to fix, at least. It might even take circuits."

Wish groans. "Circuits?"

I nod. "But look, I can set up the primary controls at a workstation. Just leave me to it and I'll get us up and running again. It'll take time but I can fix this."

Hart hums again, then nods. His head turns and then his body follows. As he whizzes out of the room, he calls back. "As I am surplus to requirements, I will return to my charging station for the duration." I blink but the doors swish closed behind him before I can call him back. He sounds carefree but I'm not sure if he thinks I called him useless. Did I hurt his feelings? Do droids even have feelings?

Wish drops the packets of food and drink on the nearest workstation and throws herself down into a chair. I take the seat beside her and turn to face the screen.

A while later, I'm lost in the lines of code again, tinkering a sub-command here and tweaking a root if-then statement there. Wish sighs heavily beside me so I pause and turn to her. "How about a reconnaissance mission?"

Her eyebrows lift and she leans toward me. "What do you have in mind?"

"Well, I'm stuck behind the interface here but I need to know more about the ship and its layout." I pull up an on-screen map that shows a sprawl of decks then push a button on the surface of the desk. With a slight hiss, a small handheld tablet slides up from inside a compartment. I swipe the map across to the tablet and it flicks from the large heads-up display to the small device. "Records indicate that some areas of the ship are damaged but there's no information about what kind of damage or the extent of it. I need you to go explore, make notes about what you find, and then flick it back to me. Here, I'll show you."

I show Wish how to enter notes, records, and markers on the map and then sync the data back to the main systems hub with an identity flag that will flash my terminal a notice. She nods, excited, and spends a few long deccas browsing the map before darting to the door. It swishes open as she approaches and I sigh, suddenly realising that a part of me had wondered if we might have been locked in. "I'll be back soon."

"Stay safe!" I call. She snaps a mock salute, clicks her heels together, and accompanies it with a cheeky wink. The door slides closed behind her.

Alone in the lab, I glance around. I feel as if I've been left unsupervised in a giant playground. Almost giddy with excitement, I spin in my chair, taking in the whole expanse of the room. The lines of text on the screen of my workstation remind me of my primary purpose, so I turn back to the base code and continue tinkering through it.

Occasionally, a bleep alerts me to an update from Wish. I respond to each of her discoveries as she explores every inch of the ship. As we work, a part of me wonders what Wish's genetic memories make familiar for her. We clearly have different instinctive interests. How can we be clones if we aren't identical?

3

Elixr

Wish

Excitement bubbles through me and I glance down at the tablet. The lift door opposite seems like it should open into another chamber but I can't find a way to activate the door. According to the schematic, it's a simple hexagonal room. It's only half the size of the lab. Niah can't even get it to unlock from the master controls in the lab so eventually we both give up. Besides, I've seen several other areas of the ship I want to explore. We can come back to this later.

I take the lift down to the next level. The doors slide open on another long corridor. Either side of me, I glimpse the edges of an overgrown garden.

I pull open a cabinet in the wall beside the entry and peer inside. It's large and looks like an empty storage closet but there's no base. There is, however, a twin set of buttons marked with up and down arrows. I push up and hear a soft swish as a platform whizzes up from lower levels of the ship and settles into place. "Cool! I wonder where it goes."

I pull up the map, noting the way the little cupboard seems to be marked on the two lower levels. There must be a section of this little lift that does a horizontal transit because its corresponding segments are in the refrigeration storage units of the main mess kitchen and the morning break room quarters. I close the doors again and turn to explore the rest of the room.

I glance around, trying to take in every detail as I move along the hexagonal path around a large chamber. The walls and ceiling are made of thick glass that looks out on the star-littered universe above. It feels like a giant greenhouse, which is odd because I imagine it doesn't get much natural light in the vast expanses between stars.

"I guess that's why the beams between the panels glow," I say to myself as I gaze up through the overhanging canopy to the ceiling above. I tap in some notes on the tablet as Niah asked me to do.

Most of the plants have sprawled in their untended state as if trying to claim the ship as their own. Even so, they are contained to the single giant room and clear of the walkway. As I turn another corner, I catch a glimpse of an inner courtyard beyond the wall of thicker trees. At its centre dances a water fountain spitting a mist of cool, clean water into the air and cascading back into a small pool at its base.

Then I see the garden rambling around it. I feel my mouth drop open. My stomach growls and I can't help but prance around the room as I gather the bright coloured fruits and vegetables. I taste and graze, feeling the rich flavours splatter my tongue. I frown as my arms fill, then sigh. "I can't carry all this." I grin as I realise exactly the purpose of the storage cupboard I'd seen earlier. Perfect!

I spend what must be several factors exploring the ship. I wonder where my place, or rather the place of my predecessor was on the ship, but none of the crew quarters feel familiar. There are areas I can't get into but, with Niah's help to bypass system locks, we manage to open most doors. Since there's so much to explore, I just skip the ones we can't open. I can come back to them later. I'd rather check out the medical lab, and the cargo bay which looks like it doubles as a hangar.

The med lab is closest to the main kitchen so, after I've transferred the food to cold storage and raided the kitchen for any other potential snacks, I head down what looks like a section of crew quarters to the large room at the end. I stop before the twin doors because there's a flashing marker on the room and the panel beside the door is also flashing red. Clearly the room is locked, but this is different to some of the other locked doors Niah helped me with.

"Niah, this one has red flashing lights."

"Hang on, I'll check."

It feels like an orbit before Niah messages again. The switch on the door lights up green as her new message beeps onto the screen.

"I needed to activate life support in the room. Should be good to go now."

The twin doors slide open and the lights in the room flicker on. I notice how clean and orderly the equipment seems to be. This place looks pristine compared to the mess of the crew quarters I walked past earlier.

Not only is it pristine, it's state-of-the-art. Floor to ceiling windows offer a panorama of the distant stars. Five medical beds sprawl around the walls to offer patients the greatest view. A larger diagnostic slab sits closer to the middle of the room.

What really draws my eye though, is the strange gentle sloshing of a pale mauve liquid in what is either a very, very big bath, or a small swimming pool. I lean down and dip my fingers in the goo. It's slightly warm and wet, but thicker than water. I trail my hand through it and feel the slight resistance of the fluid's weight.

"Niah! You really have to see this." I type, syncing the message with her workstation as she'd shown me.

"What is it?"

"There's a swimming pool in the medical lab but it doesn't use water, it's some kind of gel."

"Sounds cool, if you take a sample you can run a spec analysis on the diagnostics table. We can check out those results later."

"Sure!"

I glance around, finding the storage cupboard of medical supplies on the far wall next to the door. I draw out a test tube and take a sample of liquid. I slip it into a tube slot on the diagnostics table which seems to hum to life.

I stick my head around the door of a small bathroom, just a bathroom, and then move on to check out the rest of the ship.

By the time I reach the lowest deck, I'm hungry

again. I hijack a small satchel from one of the rooms I passed earlier and detour back through the kitchen. Now I have a small stash of food to munch as I let the lift carry me to the final floor.

I'm finishing the last bite of soft flesh from a sweet purple fruit when the doors slide open. I almost choke on the mouthful when I see the cargo bay sprawling before me. Now, this is my idea of heaven.

The bay is wide and deep with huge hangar doors. It's also decked out with the coolest mech I've ever seen. Of course, that isn't saying much since I guess I've never really seen much mech, but the echo within me that remembers a life I never lived seems just as impressed as I am.

I lay my hand on the ships and equipment. It all seems eerily familiar. I know this is called a launch wing and it's designed for defence and attack should it be necessary while in space. Those are zip gliders designed for ground transport but capable of low orbit flight and used so that the Elixr doesn't have to land too much. They can haul the huge transport pods that hang on the walls. And those are mini-zips. They can haul the pods too, but they go significantly faster when they're not hauling. They are great for quick planetary travel between points but they can't be used in space because the pilot on top is exposed to the elements.

I type it all to Niah, punctuated with several exclamation marks. She sends back a message, "*eyeroll*".

"Hey!" I type back.

"It's cool, Wish. Sorry I don't share your

enthusiasm for travel and transport units."

"You're on a space ship, Niah. Isn't that at least a little bit awesome?"

"I just want to get home."

The tablet falls silent after that. I don't know how to respond because I'd definitely rather be exploring. But I've explored most of the ship now. There are just two places I've not been able to check out. A room off of the crew quarters, and the small hexagonal room on the top floor. I head back two levels to give the crew quarter doors another go.

Niah

Long factors pass. From time to time, Wish needs help getting access to blocked parts of the ship. From my terminal, I activate doors, lights, and even, occasionally, life support systems in parts of the ship that have been deactivated.

Logs indicate that Elixr shut down a lot of key systems in response to my shutdown command earlier and, while it saves processor power, it's important to keep certain systems active. I make time to sort back through the systems. I recheck the status of most operations until I am satisfied we are running as efficiently as possible.

That means more and more often, I need to activate and deactivate parts of the ship as Wish moves through them, but it's fun to interact with her through the interface. Her text responses are frequently animated with excitement as she thrives on the curiosity of exploration and discovery. There has only been one chamber so far that is secured with multi-layer encryptions I can't break.

It is curious, but since the room indicates only storage functions, I assume it's a secure vault for the crew's valuables. Wish suggests that we can come back to it later.

I push back my chair and rise to my feet. My legs ache from sitting so long and I remember that I haven't really used them in my sixteen narcycles of life. I stretch my neck, rotate my shoulders, and flex my back.

An alert flashes up on my screen. It blinks red and white with the words "Hey Niah!" I'm startled as Wish's soft voice echoes through the room. "Niah!"

I glance around but I'm still alone. "Wish?"

"Oh, yeah, I found out how to turn on the voice exchange between our work stations. But you have to come, Niah. I need your help."

"What do you mean? Can't I do it from the console like everything else?"

"No, you really do have to come. It's too heavy for me to lift on my own."

"What?" I pull up the map. A yellow dot flickers indicating her life-sign on the display. Either side of her stretches a series of chambers marked crew quarters. A short way down the corridor is a larger chamber but it's faded out as if blocked from the system. "What is it?"

"Just come, Niah." The map zooms out and a row of directions flash into place on the screen as if Wish swiped an overlay into place. I tap the desk beside me, grab the tablet that rises up from its compartment and swipe the screen to my device before darting out the door.

I head down two levels in the vertical transport and find Wish waiting for me. She waves up and down the long column of crew quarters. "All abandoned," she says. "Full of family photos, posters, beds, and stuff. I mean they feel lived in, but there's no one here." A shiver runs over my skin as I feel the almost living loneliness of an abandoned ship. What really happened to the crew?

"What about this one?" I ask, looking around. Heavy panels from the walls and ceiling are strewn across the floor, leaning heavily against the bare metal under-frame that makes up the basic structural integrity of the ship's hull. Against the door beside Wish, a shaft of metal is jammed into place. It's wedged into the functional weight of the door so the door can't open. Against the metal are rusty smears and splatter stains. "What in the nine-voids?"

"I'm thinking something major happened. There are other signs of disruption, tossed bunks, damaged walls, raided weapons lockers, but this is the first time I've seen this." She gestures to the warping of the door. "They've jammed it shut as if they didn't want what was inside to get out. Which is odd because the map says these are the captain's quarters."

I perk up, glancing down at my screen. "Really?" More curious than ever, I clip the tablet onto a harness at my hip that seems designed to hold the portable device. Then I cross to take a closer look at the way the metal warps around the structure of the door.

"I can't shift it myself, but it does move a little.

Maybe if we both pull?"

I nod and step up beside her. I grip the panel. "One, two, three?" She nods back and on a three count we pull together. The metal plate shifts several inches but doesn't quite come free. I feel a little dizzy from the effort and pant, catching my breath.

Wish frowns at the obstruction. "Again, harder," she says.

I nod and we tug again. I stumble slightly, dropping the weight of the metal to the floor as it springs free from the door. It clangs and I jump aside so that it doesn't crush my feet.

Beside me, Wish dances back. Across from us, the door makes a loud grinding noise as if shifting on misaligned gears. "Hang on," Wish says. She leans against the door, pushing the seam to one side until it clunks and springs open as if the mechanism inside snapped.

I lift an eyebrow. "Sure you don't have super powers?"

She laughs. "It just needed a little weight. I think it was already damaged." I nod and we push the other side together before stepping over the cluttered threshold and into the room beyond.

Inside, the room is immaculate. The bed is made with military precision. The desk is tidy and functional. Blue-lit screens still flash with forgotten processes. A spinning ball of orange light with a solar map takes prominent place on the display. Opposite, the room expands into a suite with a kitchenette and en suite bathroom with modern fittings.

"Wow," Wish says. I nod.

"Nice digs huh? Dibs?" I turn to her and wink. She laughs.

"Hey, your DNA gets dibs, sure thing." A weight sinks in my belly as I register her words and I swallow.

There are signs of the captain's personality everywhere. Touches of warmth and colour give the pristine room a sense of having been someone's home. A single photograph in a frame sits on a low table beside the bed. A young honey-haired, brown-eyed woman gazes up at a smiling man. Their faces are eerily familiar.

I wander around, exploring the strange man who I guess is my predecessor. Kind of my father? With a swish, a panel opens in the wall beside the bathroom and an array of clothes springs out on a rod of hooks. There, amongst the skin-tight male-form synthetic body suits is a stylish black coat lined with navy silk interior. Its brass buttons gleam as if polished with dedication. A row of stripes panels the shoulders, and pins decorate the lapels and wrists. I reach forward, running my fingers over the fine fabric. A familiar scent dances up to me. Home. It smells like home. I reach out, tracing my hand down the sleeve.

"Put it on," Wish urges.

I glance at her and sigh. "It's a dead man's coat."

She shrugs. "Then he won't need it."

I gaze at it, longing for its familiar, warm embrace. I already know that wearing it will fill me with confidence and pride. It's a captain's coat. It commands respect. But I don't know if I've any right to expect any. I was a mistake, a malfunction.

While Hart still seems to think I can complete the mission, I can't help but wonder if his hopes are misplaced.

"Really, Niah. You should wear it. Wouldn't he want you to?"

I bite my lip. "You think so?"

She nods and after another brief moment of hesitation, I reach for the coat and pull it from the hanger. I tuck my arms through the sleeves and wrap the coat around me. It's longer than I imagined, hanging almost to my feet, but it's warm and it feels right to wear it.

A flashing light above an elongated panel draws my attention to the wall of white behind where the coat had been hanging. Down the rim of the panel is an array of scratches as if someone tried to jimmy open a compartment with a sharp metal tool. I touch the screen on the front. A warning flashes up. "Access Denied."

"What's this?"

Wish leans forward to take a look then shrugs her shoulders. "No idea."

"Do you think he tried to get it open?"

Wish shrugs again so I unclip my tablet and swish the command so that its screen lights up on the panel display. I tinker through the commands, looking for an unlock sequence. The flashing red light gets more insistent with each attempt and eventually a blasting alarm startles us both. "Eagrim's beak!" I swear, frantically pushing buttons as I try to reset the system and shut off the alerts. My heart is racing. Beside me, Wish frantically darts to the door and glances down the corridor as if terrified a crew of crazed army bots will descend to obliterate us.

"Shut it up, Niah! Before we get in trouble."

"I'm trying!" I frantically press commands and retype lines of code.

"Uh oh!" I turn at the groan of bored frustration Wish makes. "It's the bossy bot."

Hart whizzes into the room. "Cease! Cease! What are you doing? You are not permitted to access that system. Desist immediately!"

4

Mission Revealed

Niah

Behind Hart's manic bluster, Wish is making exaggerated gestures and I try not to laugh. The robot seems to be on a rather pronounced tirade so I wait, wondering if he'll run himself out of battery or blow a circuit.

"You should not be here. These are the private quarters of Captain Bellamy. What are you doing? You should not touch his things. These are the private quarters of Captain Bellamy. You are not Captain Bellamy. You may share a remarkable passing likeness and genetic material but you are not the captain. You are a sleeper. You will only become necessary once we have returned to Nar. Why are you in here? You should not be in here. You should not touch his things. These are the private quarters of Captain Bellamy." His litany of reprimands winds to a stop and he falls silent. Then he blinks and glances at the open closet behind me and the secret compartment within.

"NO!" he cries.

The bot zips over and attempts to slam the panel across the closet. The bar protruding from the wall catches him about the head as he reaches around it to pull the panel from its slot in the wall. Hart huffs as he starts pushing buttons on the control panel trying to figure out how to retract and re-secure the clothes locker.

Seeing his clunky fingers working all sorts of wrong commands on the screen I reach past him and nudge his hands out of the way. After three precise clicks the pole slides back into the wall, taking what remains of Bellamy's clothing with it. The panel slides across and it clicks into place, locked.

"Satisfied?" I ask. Hart turns toward me. His head tilts down and then up as if he's looking me over. A small ring pops up on his face screen beneath his eyes.

A soft hiss sounds from him. "What are you wearing?"

I remember the heavy drape of the coat over my shoulders and go to shrug it off with a guilty grimace. "I'm sorry, I shouldn't have touched it."

Hart reaches his metal fingers out and places his hand on my shoulder. He halts the material before I can pull it down my arms. "No," he says. "Leave it on. It suits you."

I furrow my brow, confused by the odd light of reflection that seems to flicker in Hart's features. The tilt of his head, the shimmer of brightness around the lights of his eyes. The image of a single teardrop slides down the screen. "Emotion?" I ask.

He hums, then shakes his head. "Of course not. Such emotional response is not computable."

"But that was a tear, Hart. You really cared about him, didn't you?"

"My captain was a good man," Hart blustered. "He didn't deserve–" He pauses and shakes his head, then turns away. His shoulders tilt forward in what could be considered a slump as he slowly sways toward the door. As he reaches it, he turns back and looks up at me. His eyes are expressionless orbs again. "Have you completed the repairs?"

I swallow and shake my head. I feel smaller and smaller as he keeps his gaze fixed on me. Beside him, Wish shifts from foot to foot. "Oh, come on, Hart. We weren't doing any harm."

His head turns toward her and his eyes blink. "You have no reason to be here. If you are not repairing the ship then you are unnecessary to its function and should return to your sleeping pod."

Wish and I both shudder. I shake my head and cross the room. "I'm going back to the lab."

"Me too." Wish falls in beside me. We walk back, heads down, as we navigate the debris-strewn corridor. When we reach the junction, I glance left and then right trying to remember the way I'd come. "That way," Wish says, pointing to the heavy metal doors of the lift. We step inside and zoom up two floors. Wish leads the way back down the long corridor.

Before we reach the lab I turn to Hart, who is trailing behind us like a prison guard ensuring his charges do not stray. The droid lifts up as if startled as he comes to a halt before me. His head tilts back and he gazes up at me.

"Hart, the processor units are stored on the next floor down, aren't they?" I ask.

His blue orbs blink and he nods. "Yes, come and see."

He turns back to the lift and guides us down one floor and along a long corridor similar to the one that leads to the lab. When the doors swish open, we enter a similarly shaped room. This one is arrayed in a series of spiralling columns that run the length of the floor to ceiling. Some offer a warm hum that sounds like normal function. Others are completely black, silent, and cold. Two have mild static sparks. And one is creating a strange hissing static that sounds like the garbled chatter of a whispered alien language.

Wish leans close. "What is that?"

Hart's chassis lifts as if he's shrugging his shoulders. "They are damaged and non-functioning."

I wander around the consoles. Occasionally, I plug in my tablet and navigate through the base code that runs these processors, links them to each other, and stores the vital archives and access memory that keeps the system running. It's difficult because even linking my device to the network creates a hanging stall that maxes out the memory functions for several long ticks. Thankfully, most of the processors are fully functional.

I keep my distance as I approach the two setting off static. I look carefully over the devices, wondering where the contact points are and if there might be a safe way to uncouple the power so that they're both not dangerously live. They're draining power and processor speed from the overall system. As I crouch close to the floor, I see it, a series of frazzled wires crossing each other. I sigh, then stand and turn to Hart.

"I can probably fix these two but I'll need some tools." He blinks, or at least I expect him to, but instead the twin orbs wink shut and his face screen blinks out altogether. I startle. "Hart?" He doesn't respond.

"Hart?" Wish echoes. She's standing beside him so jostles his shoulder. He remains silent and dark. "Hart, wake up!" Wish gives him a shake and his body glides smoothly back and forth.

"Oh? What?" He blusters, blinking back to life. "Is there an earthquake?"

Wish takes a deep breath. "You spaced out on us for a moment there."

His head tilts. "I did? Oh dear. I do apologise. Were you saying something?"

I stare at him a long moment, wondering exactly what is going on with him. In fact, I'm staring so long that eventually the odd little eyebrow light pops up on his face screen. "Oh!" I say, remembering my original point. "I was saying that if I had the right tools, I could fix this."

"The fabrication database has an extensive storage of three-dimensional design specifications. But it requires processing capacity and is currently offline. The crew uses the drive to fabricate and then deconstruct as necessity dictates. Does necessity dictate?"

I nod. "Yes. Can you show me the fabrication database?"

"The fabricator is in the lab. Come on."

He spins about to dart off down the corridor again so I call out, "Wait!" His head turns back to me, and then his body. "We'll get to that next, but I just want to check over these last units so I can decide how to fix them. They might be easier to bring online."

I trace over the four silent units and carefully adjust the wires and switches so that they match those on the fifteen working units. I plug my tablet into each one but nothing happens. "Elixr?"

"Yes, November-One-Alpha-Four?"

"It's Niah. Can you do a systems check to tell me if power is getting through the circuits to units three, nine, thirteen, and sixteen?"

A long moment passes and I'm about to check in to see if she heard my command when the unit in front of me lights up and starts hissing. I jump back, afraid it might spark, but the static hiss dips into a series of clicks and beeps as it powers up. I glance down at my tablet to see the reboot commands running default diagnostics as the unit comes back online. The code is clean and in about two deccas the system starts humming along with the other functional units.

"Power restored to unit thirteen."

I smile. "Thank you Elixr, and the others?"

"Processing."

She falls silent again so I wait to see if any of the others come back online. Suddenly an arc of electricity jettisons from unit three. I jump back as it sparks across to nine. The electrical contact flares, singeing a black-edged hole through the unit's interface.

"Oops!" says the soft feminine voice of the ship. Wish chuckles and I can't help feeling a wry sense of humour.

"Oops?"

"Error, systems malfunction in processor room."

I laugh. "Yeah, we got that Elixr. So, I'm guessing there is an electrical fault with three?"

"And nine has sustained damage."

I sigh. "Yeah, I'll say." I step up to the unit and examine the components. The damage is relatively isolated on the surface, although there's no way to really know if it has blown the circuits inside. I peel back the outer shell casing. Most of the interior looks okay. "Elixr, can you initiate the cooling fan on nine?"

"Processing."

A slight hiss sounds from the unit and the interface sparks with small flickers of electricity as if the display is trying to light up. I carefully plug my tablet into the unit and it shows the start-up diagnostics which registers the damage and lists several other interior parts. I sigh. It's going to take factors to fix and that's assuming the fabricator can make these parts.

I manually power down the unit and turn to the last of the four. "Okay, Elixr, what about sixteen?"

I step back from the unit, not sure if it might arc. Hart watches from a distance and I half suspect he's afraid it will arc in his direction when the power comes on. Metal to metal. But long deccas pass and nothing happens.

"Elixr?"

"Three concurrent tests indicate a systematic failure in the power coupling between units sixteen and seventeen. Power is unable to feed through the system."

"So, it's bypassing the unit?" I ask, my brow furrowed as I try to make sense of the odd coupling behaviour.

"Affirmative."

"Where is that coupling located?"

"Processing."

Moments later a panel in the deck of the room slides open and reveals a chunk of thick cord. Three coupling units are linked together but one sits oddly in its socket. "Elixr, power down all electricity through this coupling station."

"Affirmative."

I reach in and pull the unit out. It's fitted with a strange connection that seems to create a stranglehold on the cord. "What–" I peer carefully down at the pieces which fit together in intricate locks. With careful fingers, I twist the sequence through a series of pressure points and it unlocks, clattering into the compartment below. I reach down and pick it up. I look over the odd device and wonder what it could possibly have been intended to do besides straightjacket the power into processor sixteen.

I recouple the two cords and set them back in their socket in the bay then sit back. "Okay, try it again, Elixr." The unit hums to life, proceeds through its start-up diagnostics and connection beeps and clicks, then settles into smooth pattern with the other functioning units. I get up and plug in my tablet. "Everything looks normal. Wait–"

It's gone almost as soon as I see it but flickers back in a staggered pattern. I count the beats and time it so that I can press the strange symbol before it disappears again. As the lines of code start scrolling the screen, I feel a sense of dread and my breath shudders from my body. "Elixr eliminate power to sixteen immediately." The screen goes black. "Run diagnostics on one through fifteen."

"Processing."

"What was it?" Wish asks, peering over my shoulder.

I shake my head. "I'm not sure, but it definitely didn't look friendly. I think someone planted a virus in this processor."

"A virus? What would that do?"

I unplug my tablet and run a quick diagnostic check. It's clean, thank goodness. "I don't know. But I'm going to have to detach the unit from everything else so that I can safely take a closer look."

Hart hovers close. "Will that get Elixr fully functional?"

"She should already be running more smoothly. We got a couple of units back online and I'm pretty confident that I can fix at least these three."

Wish waves at the unit she's been examining. Its strange static hiss still pulses from the column. "What about this one?"

I plug in my tablet and browse through the

interface, checking the databanks as I run diagnostics. "It's running at capacity, although it doesn't seem to be doing anything in particular. It's–" I push a few commands on my tablet. "I think the static is a distress signal."

"A distress signal?"

"That's what it says in the file names. It's a series of audio files marked as warnings and distress."

"But I can't hear anything."

"I know. But–" I listen. Within the odd static are fractions of variating irregularities. "Non-mechanic."

"What?"

"It's too imperfect. I think these are Narian vocal patterns."

"Can you filter it so that we can understand?"

"Not from here. I could probably build a three-dimensional translator blueprint for the fabricator if I had enough time."

Hart bleeps. "Time, time. We have all the time in Nar, and none. Will listening to radio voices get Elixr running at full capacity so that we can resume our return trip to Nar?"

Wish looks shattered as she realises the answer is probably no. I think on it a moment then respond, "What if the distress signal can tell us what went wrong with the ship the first time? What happened to the crew? Is it really safe to return to Nar if we're bringing something with us that could destroy everything?"

The blue orbs of Hart's eyes widen and a small O-ring appears as his mouth. "No! We must return to fulfil our mission! We must bring back the cure!

We must save Nar, not destroy it!"

Wish turns to him. "Then we better make the time to check out this message."

I touch her shoulder. "I think we can make headway on both. The fabricator should function now. I'll repair the other units and we can get navigation back online to replot the course. Then, while we travel, we can work out the static."

Wish

Niah gets so lost in her work that she forgets I'm even here. I sit for a time, watching her move between her workstation and the fabricator. It's pretty boring stuff. I wish I could help but I don't think there's anything I can do.

With a sigh, I spin in the chair in front of this desk for a while. The map on the tablet flickers but I've seen most of the ship now. I pull out a ration bar and place the tablet on the workstation. The large holo-screen flickers to life and I blink at the user interface. On the flat of the desk a series of keys and inputs are glowing.

I glance back at Niah but she's absorbed in what she's doing. I turn back to the display. "What harm is there in exploring a little?" I mutter. Niah doesn't even hear me.

Most of the machine is pretty boring. I come across a couple of games and spend a little while on each. There's not much to them but at least it's passing the time. Anything is better than Hart breathing down my neck about how useless I am.

Still, there's only so many times you can win

before even that gets tiresome. Instead, I begin digging into the ship's archives. They date back dozens of narcycles, maybe hundreds. It's a treasure trove of interesting facts about the crew, the ship, and even about Nar. I dig around, hunting for something familiar, wondering if I'll ever find myself among the ship's crew.

I could spend several factors here. I munch on another ration bar as I scroll through some of the documents. Everything is here, an archive of the ship's entire history. "Now this could get interesting."

5

Secrets In The Static

Niah

The parts actually come together really easily. The fabricator is a dream to work with and the three-dimensional manipulation and construction program is almost instinctive. Although the repairs take several factors, I do eventually bring more of the processors back online. I measure the processor capacity with the new systems active and notice, finally, that there is a degree of buffer. "Elixr?"

"Yes, Captain."

I grimace. "Don't call me that. Can you bring up navigation?"

"Would you like me activate Harttade and bring him online to manage our navigation systems?"

I sigh. "Yeah, call him up. I think we should be able to get back online now and replot the course."

"Affirmative. Replotting."

Moments later the doors open and Hart blusters in. "Waking sleeping robots. What in the nine-voids has this universe come to? Will I ever reach full charge capacity again?"

I ignore him, instead focusing on bringing the ship about. "Elixr? Do we have a course?"

"Affirmative November-One-Alpha-Four. Course set for Nar. Seventeen jumps and twenty-four factors to destination."

"What does that mean?" Wish asks.

Hart sighs. "Nearly home. Did you uncover the message?"

I turn to Hart. "Not yet."

Wish leans forward in her chair. "What are 'jumps'?"

"The ship is fitted with a jump drive, it is the most efficient way to travel great distances," I tell her, then turn back to Hart, "And it uses both a lot of power and a lot of processor, right?"

"Of course. It's a jump drive." Two lines above his eye orbs tip down as if he's considering how stupid I must be.

"Bear with me." I turn back to the walls, looking up at them as if facing the disembodied voice that is the ship's verbal response unit. "Elixr, initiate return course but do not activate the jump drive."

"Calculating. Return trip will take five million, three hundred and twenty-three thousand, eight hundred and sixty-nine point two five narcycles without jump drive."

"I know, we're not going to never use it, I just want to make sure as many processors are online as possible and test the power capacity of the ship before we use the jump drive."

There's a soft hum from Hart as he mutters. "Girl clone baby telling me how to fly my own ship as if

I'm not a state-of-the-art telemetry unit whose whole purpose is to fly the ship. Even my own captain let me fly the ship the way I'm supposed to fly the ship." His muttering continues so I reach a hand out to him.

"Sorry Hart, can you take it from here?"

His head perks up and his eyes blink. "Affirmative! Elixr, transfer navigation controls."

"Navigation transferred to hybrid autonomous research, telemetry, teleportation, and defence engine."

Hart raises his hands, taking the invisible wheel again. The shift as the ship accelerates and turns creates a slight rock within the room and I remember the inertial dampeners are still not at capacity. Suddenly, I'm very thankful we're not using the jump drive because without those dampeners the creation of the slipstream could have been very, very messy. Not to mention, reminding me to check that the shields will be capable of sustaining warp. "Easy does it okay, Hart? I'll get us up and running at best capacity soon but for now keep her light and steady."

He nods his head and wanders back through the door and down the corridor, steering the ship the whole way with a happy hum and a trail of pink tendrils in his jet stream.

I turn back to the fabricator. There's more I could do with the processors on the next level but Wish is still lingering. She's been trolling through the database at a nearby workstation. I imagine she must be pretty bored, so I decide to first focus on creating something to help us translate the static.

"Let's get you some static to translate." I smile and she nods, coming to join me at the fabricator.

After fabricating the tools I need, I find it easier and easier to understand how to manipulate the program and manufacture a device that can record, filter, process, and relay the static. When it's crafted, it looks a bit like a ham radio. I wonder how I know to think of its shape like that or what name to call it. It's strange to have these old memories that are clear and not clear at the same time. It's like looking through a foggy window but knowing with certainty what's on the other side.

"So, what will this do?" Wish asks.

"Okay, so first it will record the output from the unit. You plug it in directly so that rather than recording the garbled version we're hearing, it will receive a true transfer from the system directly."

"Like plugging a speaker into a mic jack?"

I glance up at her and furrow my brow. "What?"

"Music?"

"I don't know, do sound systems work that way?"

Wish shrugs.

"Anyway, the device will unpack the files and run a series of tweaks over things so that eventually it should filter down to better and better quality."

"Tweaks?"

"What? Do you want me to get all fancy and technical? It's high-tech. Just go with me, okay? Basically, it makes the bad sound good. But it takes time and requires monitoring so that you can micro-adjust as it makes changes. You let it know when its changes are good and when the quality gets worse, you adjust."

"Oh, okay. So, I listen, tweak, and eventually we get good audio." She winks, straddling her chair. I roll my eyes and chuckle.

"Right, just get to work already, would you? I'm going to go downstairs and get those other processors back online. I'll be back in a bit."

It takes about four factors to deal with the processors but since Wish doesn't ping my tablet, I figure she's either fallen asleep in her chair or wandered off to continue exploring the ship now Hart is happily ensconced on the bridge. Or maybe she's still processing the audio.

I run a final diagnostic on the now functioning processors. Most are running at full capacity again. The shields are secure and their scripts function with precise calculations to minimise power consumption, which is actually pretty impressive from a programming perspective. I grin, feeling an odd sense of pride that I don't understand since I didn't have any part in the ship's original design. There are some remaining kinks in the processing speed, signs of age perhaps, not to mention the processor I left offline because of the virus, but the remaining systems are running the best they'll be without doing a major overhaul. I pat the last unit and stretch my back. I run one last check over power; it's smooth, even, and well balanced. "As good as it's going to get. Elixr?"

"Yes nine-alpha-one-four."

I grimace. "Would you please call me Niah?"

"Yes, Niah."

"We're up to capacity so I think it's safe to raise the inertial dampener levels, activate the warp shield, and incorporate those jumps into our navigation now. Can you let Hart know?"

"Affirmative."

She falls silent again so I assume it's happening and head back up to the lab.

As I walk through the door, I see Wish leaning close to the unit, her eyes fixed on the device and ears covered in a headset.

"Where did you get that?"

She doesn't respond and I realise she probably can't hear me. I step close and lift an earpiece from her ear. She startles back, almost falling from her chair with a gasp.

"Eagrim's beak! You scared me." She blinks then looks confused. "I think eagrims are some sort of bird, but they don't even have beaks. It's so weird having fragments of memory that aren't even mine."

I nod because I've felt the same strange sense, as if my brain holds two minds instead of one.

"Did you get anywhere?"

"Actually, yeah. Listen!" She taps a few of the keys on the interface on her desk and a soft whooshing noise fills the room. I glance down and realise she's hooked the radio up to the main computer.

A rich, warm voice breaks through the hissing static. It's eerily familiar and yet strangely alien. "They're losing control! Mayday! The Elixr has been sabotaged, the crew is in mutiny. They're losing control." The static arcs up again and the next section of the recording is lost but then it resumes. "–in my room. The cure is secure. I have hidden a data record that contains the fundamental structure required for fabrication in my own quarters. But I fear it is not safe. I feel myself slipping away. Just like the others, it starts with headaches and sickness. Disequilibrium. I am infected and I fear I may succumb. To ensure the safety of our mission, I have inserted a priority status statement into Harttade and programmed Elixr to follow the base command to return home. I can no longer restore Nar myself. I cannot allow this sickness to infect our home." His voice pauses for a long moment. "Forgive me. You are our only hope. There was no other choice." And then the voice fades and the static returns.

I swallow, then release a slow, shuddered sigh and glance over at Wish. She's watching me so closely as if waiting for me to say something, but I don't know how to respond. A lot of the message didn't make sense but the dread in the pit of my stomach is very, very real.

"Baull-scat," I say and she nods.

"Yeah."

Niah

"So, the cure is in that locker, right?"

"The plans for it at least. That's what it sounds like."

"And Hart said that we're supposed to have something to do with the cure. At least you are."

"Hart doesn't seem to know much of anything. If

he does have a primary mission protocol–" I fall silent and Wish nods beside me.

"Something has screwballed his memory and prevents him from being able to access it."

"Or he won't tell us." I pace the room, circling the fabrication unit in the middle. "Look," I say. "I got most of the processors online and we're back on track. Let's just see how it plays out when we get there."

Wish shakes her head. "Niah, I have to tell you something but I don't want you to freak out. I'm freaked out enough for both of us."

"What is it?"

"Well, before I started tinkering with the static, you know, while you were getting the sublight and navigation back up so we could at least get moving? Anyway, I was going over some of the old archives in the main database. There are records dating back hundreds of narcycles. It talks about the original fleet that set out on this quest, this mission we're on, to save Nar."

I feel that pit in my stomach again and bite my lip. Then, taking a breath, I cross to sit in the chair beside her. It's probably best I sit down for this.

"Yes?"

"So, Captain Bellamy and the crew of the Elixr took off from Nar over two hundred narcycles ago with a fleet of seven ships. They were sent to a long distant sector of the galaxy in search of what they called the Cure of Shadows. Apparently some professor, like Bellamy's dad or brother or something, invented a tech that poisoned the planet. I think it's a bit like radiation, except it affected the way light refracts or something. I don't really get it."

I listened carefully, trying to pick out the most important aspects of what Wish was saying. The story tumbled out of her in a rush.

"Anyway," Wish continued, "Captain Bellamy – his name was Jacob and he sounds pretty amazing – well, he was sent out to bring back something to fix it. The professor stayed behind to do what he could to protect what was left of the planet but the records don't really say much about that. I guess because the ships left so they don't know what happened." She pauses to breathe, then gazes across at me. "Say something."

"Processing." I say, mimicking Elixr. Wish laughs but continues to watch me, waiting. "No really," I say, "it's just a bit mind blowing. So, okay. If we put that together with what Captain Bellamy said in his recording we can say they must have reached their destination and found the 'cure'?" Wish nods. "But then something happened that made the crew and everyone…"

I trail off because, although I don't know exactly what happened to them, it's not hard to guess that they must be dead. We haven't seen any bodies, but the crew quarters had been trashed. There were traces of blood and damage.

Wish dips her head, looking at her hands. She's twisting her fingers in her lap. She whispers, "He jettisoned them."

I swallow, not sure I want to believe it. "What?"

"The ship logged it. Shortly after the timestamp of that audio there is a ship-wide vacuum to space.

Even his own quarters. I think that's what he meant, you know, about being sorry."

"But he said, 'You are our only hope.' As if he was sorry for putting the burden on someone else."

Wish slides a dial and pushes a button. Captain Bellamy's voice fills the room again. "Forgive me." And I feel the pause in his words. "You are our only hope." Pause. "There was no other choice."

Wish switches it off again. "Three distinct statements, Niah. I think he's apologising for a lot more than that."

I nod. "We need to find out the whole story."

She nods in agreement. "We need to open that locker. Maybe there's more on that data unit."

"We'll go get it together when Hart returns to his charging station tonight.

She nods again. "Okay, tonight."

6

Scrambled Circuits

Wish

I feel pretty bad for Niah. She's been in a funk for factors now and I kind of regret telling her what Bellamy did. She has this strange kinship with the dead man. It's like she carries his guilt on her shoulders. Still, there's nothing much I can do about that.

Hart is being his usual stubborn, inconsiderate self. Niah grows more insistent. "We're not sleepers any more, Hart. Can't we stay in the crew quarters now that we're awake? We're almost back to Nar after all."

The droid tilts his head at Niah as if considering her words but then straightens. His twin orb eyes blink in place and I wonder if the bolt trap even has a clue what we're saying.

"Come on, Hart. Stop being such a downer. We just want to bunk in comfy quarters for the night. Those sleeper pods aren't exactly the height of luxury. They feel like morgue slabs."

Hart turns his dead stare on me. "You are sleepers. Those are your quarters."

Niah puts a hand on his shoulder and his head swivels to her. "But surely at some point we inherit the quarters of our predecessors."

Hart seems to consider this a moment then shakes his head. "Your duty does not require an adjustment in your sleeping quarters."

He leads us down the corridor toward Niah's room. I glance behind us. The room I woke up in is all the way at the other end of the ship, beyond the lift. I bite my lip. "Can we at least be together?"

Hart turns to me again. "Sleeper quarters are only equipped with a single pod."

"I know that! That's why we thought we could move to the crew quarters. I saw some rooms had twin share." That annoying eyebrow quirk above one of his orbs lifts and I sigh. "Come on, Hart. Lighten up will you? We've been alone and asleep for narcycles. Can't you understand that we don't want to be alone anymore?"

His eyebrow disappears and his orbs blink. An odd rumble hisses from his chassis. "Your emotional response is not computable."

"I know, it doesn't make sense–" I gear up to rant at him but Niah puts a hand on my shoulder so I turn to her. She keeps her focus on the droid.

"Hart, you haven't really explained about our mission. What more do you know of it?"

He looks as if the question startles him. I wonder if he's trying to formulate a lie. Do droids lie?

He turns away to continue leading us down the hall so I grab his arm, pulling him to a stop. He spins to face me. "Why don't you tell us anything?" I demand, leaning close. He splutters. "You can't just use us like this! We're people, you know?" Niah puts her hand on my arm again but I shake her off and turn to her. "How can you be so calm about all this baull-scat? He's just using you. Don't you see that?"

Hart blusters, "But, your mission."

"It was never OUR mission, Hart! It was Captain Bellamy's mission and he's dead. He and his whole crew threw away their lives on some pipe dream. That doesn't mean Niah and I have to do the same."

"But, you must return to Nar. You must save it!"

"Why?"

He blinks and I want to throw my fist through the stupid screen of his face. Those features seem to communicate so much but it's all just a program. Like everything else on this ship, Hart's just a fabrication of someone's greater plan for our lives.

"You must return to Nar with the cure."

"What is the cure, Hart? Do you know? Do you even know what's happened on the planet? It's been more than two hundred narcycles. Maybe there's nothing to go back to!"

I hate the pit of guilt in my stomach as the soft pink of his hover jets fade to a pale blue-green. His head dips and he turns away. "We must complete the mission."

"You don't even know what we're going back to, do you?"

"The Captain—"

"Eagrim's beak, Hart! Niah's the closest thing we have to a captain. You said so yourself. But you won't even let her, let either of us, sleep on a real bed. Are we just machines to you?"

"Wish," Niah whispers. She rubs her head and I feel instantly ashamed. She's worked so hard, for so long. She must be exhausted and all I can do is rant and rave about how unfair all this is. It's most unfair to her. She turns to Hart. "Can we at least be in the sleeper bays beside each other?"

He huffs, as if disgruntled, and I wonder how he manages to snort without a nose. He's so self-important. I grind my teeth but keep my mouth shut. He pauses at the door to the cell beside Niah's and makes a noise as if clearing his throat.

Niah turns to me. "Please, Wish. Remember the plan." She pauses, meaningfully, and it takes me a moment to remember what she's talking about. Then it clicks. We aren't planning to stay in our cells tonight. We have other things to do.

"Oh!" I nod. "I remember."

Niah

Although we aren't able to convince Hart to lighten up about our accommodations, he does let Wish use the room directly beside mine rather than the one at the other end of the ship where she'd first awoken.

"You're right, I'm tired." Wish feigns a yawn.

Hart hums. "Yes, you must sleep. Your frail Narian forms were not designed to sustain long periods of activity. You have been awake thirty-six factors. You need rest."

Hart stands back after shepherding Wish into her

room and closes the door. She leans up against the glass window and calls, "You'll wake me up, right?"

I nod. Even I can see how wiped out she looks. The dark shadows under her eyes make her pale skin more pronounced. I imagine I must look the same, but every time Hart mentions sleep, my heart pounds and I want to scream and run. Instead, I swallow the anxiety and clench my hands, drawing a sharp breath.

Hart leads me to the next door and I step inside. We can't really argue with the droid. Although I'm not sure what he could do to us, I wouldn't be surprised if he'd consider giving us an electric jolt to knock us out, and I'd rather keep my wits about me. Besides, we're not actually planning to stay confined to quarters tonight. I turn and watch the door close behind me. It clicks with a resolute lock and I frown.

"Did he just lock us in?" Wish's voice asks through the tablet still clipped to my hip. I lift the screen and see her face looking at me through the glass. "Oh, video." She winks. "Cool tech, huh? So, can you get us out of here?"

"Let's give Hart some time to wind down, but yeah, I can probably get us out of here."

We both settle back. Wish lies down on the sleeping pod but I can't bring myself to go near mine. Instead, I sit with my back to the wall beside the door and listen to the gentle sway of Wish's breath as she falls asleep. I tinker with my tablet, browsing through the archives we set up for remote access earlier in the circuit.

City Of Light

There are video logs and journal entries from Elixr's crew. My heart aches as I browse them. Some of the faces feel familiar. I sense deep friendships, long camaraderies, companions among these strangers' faces. There's a clear sense of community, of love, between these people who worked together for so long.

From the logs, it's clear they grew up together. They grew old together. When one grew nearer death, a new self, a perfect clone, was created to live that life again until the mission could be completed. They lived entire lifetimes on a ship destined to save the world. Each lifetime a perfect replica of their last. No mistakes, no genetic flaws like mine.

I swallow, feeling the weight of it all resting on my shoulders. I don't even know these people, but Wish and I, Hart and Elixr, we are all that's left of a centuries old mission. We are the only ones who can bring back the cure to save what remains of our people. If anything remains at all.

A few factors pass as Wish naps and I browse through the records. One in particular causes an ache deep in my heart. I linger on it, watching the eerily familiar face.

He looks like Wish, but he isn't. His soft smile doesn't reach the sad shadows in his eyes. The video snippet is a fragment. It looks like it once belonged to a longer log but I can't find a way to restore the rest of the entry. Instead, all I catch are a handful of words.

Deep in my gut, I sense a good man. A kind, caring, fun-loving man. "Good luck, brother," the man says. His voice is thick with true admiration, real brotherly love. Then he casts his eyes down as if wounded and in pain. When he looks up again, gazing directly at me through the screen, his eyes are laced in haunted shadows of regret. "I'm sorry," he whispers.

I know his heart is breaking. Mine is, too. I feel Bellamy's pain all over again. Torn away from a brother he truly loved. "Oli," I whisper, feeling the name on the edges of memories I can't quite grasp.

"Niah?" Wish asks and I startle because I hadn't realised she'd woken up.

"Yeah?" I swallow to clear my throat.

"Are we ready?"

I glance around at the empty room around me. I nod even though I don't have the video mode turned on so she can't actually see me. "Yeah, let's do this." I hook my tablet into the door controls and override the lock within ticks. Child's play. The door slides open and I let Wish out of her cell. "Now, we must be quiet while we deal with Hart. I don't want him to wake up."

She nods and we make our way down the corridor to his charging station. Hart is jacked in with his controls set to "powered down" mode. I carefully hook my tablet to his charging station. I lower the parameters on his alert statuses and, just to be safe, add a subcommand that will prevent him from waking up until I reset his system.

"Right, all set." I say. Hart remains inert.

Wish releases a breath. "Come on then."

We jog through the ship to Bellamy's quarters. The room looks exactly as we left it. I nudge open the closet again and set to work on the electronic lock securing the wall safe inside. It's complex, but I can't help but feel Bellamy could have hacked this himself. Why did he resort to trying to open it by force? Was his mind so far gone in his final hours?

The door pings as it finally releases and opens. Wish cheers, "Yes! You got it." I reach forward and pick up the small clear disk of glass that rests on the base of the safe. "Do you think that's it?" Wish asks.

"I imagine so." I glance around the room, wondering how to read the disk. Instinctively, my gaze is drawn to a panel on the wall beside another large screen display, currently dark. I cross the room and slip the disk into the small groove. The screen flickers to life with a series of blueprint designs. I examine them closely, piecing together the machine's function.

"What is it?"

"Some kind of dispersal unit. It's designed to cause Elixr's warp shield to emit a unique pulse seeded with some kind of liquid particles that are stored in the ship. They constructed this device but the fabrication drive lacks the orkrane needed to make the plasma it requires." I tap my tablet and run a search, then sigh in relief. "It's a mineral that's found on Nar. So I guess they always intended to finish the machine after they got home."

I flip through the file archive on the drive via the interface on the wall. Along with the plans for the cure, I find the programming structure of Hart and Elixr's final commands from Bellamy. I scan through them. Elixr's are relatively straightforward. She's programmed to run in defensive evasive mode with a self-correcting home course that will guide the ship home should no telemetry unit be available to navigate. Hart's program is much more detailed. I gasp.

"What is it?" Wish asks.

"Apparently, Hart is programmed with a series of commands and a full historical knowledge of the original fleet, their crew, their mission, and the way to administer the cure when they return."

"Why hasn't he told us any of this then?"

I shake my head. "I saw Hart's internals earlier when I scrambled his alert signals. None of this is in the main directories for access. Something must have scrambled his memory drivers."

"Is that why he spaces out?"

"Probably. If he attempts to access data that should be stored in those pockets he might be hitting erase points and getting no data. Like walking through a doorway and forgetting what you went into the room to do."

"I hate when that happens. So, is there a way to unscramble Hart's brains?"

I shut down the screen and eject the disk, tucking it into the sleeve of my suit, then turn to Wish. "I don't know, but let's say we go try." She grins at me as if it's all a fascinating adventure. I feel a similar tingle of anticipation. With every breath we're getting closer to Nar. I know it. And I can't help feeling like maybe our lives are just about to begin.

7

Brace For Impact

Niah

I've spent probably a factor trying to uncover the wiggly data files that are strewn through Hart's memory units. Some are wiped, others moved, and quite a few are damaged. I frown, growing more and more frustrated. "This is so stupid."

"What?" Wish asks.

"It might just be easier to revert his systems. I mean, that's risky too because it's possible that his backups predate the data transfer Captain Bellamy gave him before–" I stop, unable to bring myself to say the words. "Well, you know, before."

Wish nods. "What would happen if you reset him and they're not there?"

"Then we'd lose– No, wait, I'll do a full system backup of Hart's data banks directly into Elixr. Then I can do a reset and if his backup does predate the transfer, we can at least restore him to this."

"Wouldn't having him reset be better than having

him damaged?"

I bite my lip. "I don't know. He might not be the same after."

"But he'd be how he was supposed to be. The way he was before Captain Bellamy, you know?"

I nod. "Yeah. But I'd rather have the contingent. You know, just in case. I mean if he doesn't have any of his current memories, then he might not even know who or what we are."

Her mouth drops open. "Oh, yeah, that could be bad." I nod, then turn my attention to the droid. I hook him directly into the ship's server, then run a subcommand to rapid compress and transfer his data into an isolated compartment in the ship's memory.

Elixr's voice comes through the walls around us. "Oh! That tickles. What are you doing?"

I flush guiltily, then feel silly for feeling like I've lifted the ship's skirt. "Just a temporary storage, Elixr, nothing to worry about. Can we run silent for a bit so I can concentrate?"

"Affirmative." Her voice disappears and the quiet is reassuring because I really don't want Hart coming online before I can get him through a full reboot and check over his systems again.

Once the transfer is complete, I run a sweep and then shut him down. The ever-present hum of his hover jets ceases and Wish gasps, then sweeps forward to catch him before his body falls to the floor. "Um... Oops?" I say.

She laughs and shakes her head. "Niah! I'm guessing we didn't think through every aspect of this."

I shrug. "Yeah, but good catch!" I grin, then reboot from backup. His systems come back online one by one, although his hover jets don't reactivate on their own. I breathe a sigh of relief as I recognise his drives are intact and fully functioning again. I run a final line of code and include a subcommand from my tablet that should reactivate all of his active commands. He's supposed to return to full function based on his active subroutines but even with the command executed, he doesn't bluster to life like I expect.

"Something's wrong, isn't it?"

"I don't–"

We're both thrown across the small compartment. Wish clutches Hart close to her chest and then we look at each other. "Baull scat!" she swears. "What did you do, Niah?"

I swallow and shake my head. "I don't think I did that." I start feeling queasy as the ship rocks and I feel a tug against my skin as if we're spiralling out of control. I quickly tap through several more commands, trying to bring Hart back online, and shout up at the walls. "Elixr, what in the nine-voids happened?"

"I have experienced a collision event." Elixr's voice is calm, almost cheerful.

"What the void did we hit?"

"Nar's first moon." My jaw drops open and I see Wish's expression echo my own.

"Say again?"

"We experienced a glancing impact event with Nar's first moon and are now on an uncontrolled velocity approach to the planet. Would you like me to initiate a jump?"

"What? No, don't jump! Eagrim's beak! We do not want to cause a warp that would obliterate the planet. Can you course correct and veer away?"

"Negative. Sublight drives are offline and I appear to have lost two propulsion units from the starboard side."

"Baull's beast. Come on Hart, get back online." I slam another line of code through his system, overriding his systematic start-up and forcing an immediate alert and response feature. His pale blue orbs blink open and he gazes up at Wish.

His head tilts. "Why am I horizontal?"

"Oh, thank the nine-voids." Wish says, giving the droid a hug. He blinks. As Wish pulls away, his body tilts and his hover jets hum with a tinkling of pink and blue light.

"High velocity impact in thirty-seven point two deccas." Elixr's voice says calmly, as if the news she was delivering had nothing at all to do with our imminent deaths.

The small round orb of Hart's shocked mouth beams onto his face. "Transfer navigation controls!"

"Transferred."

"Damage report!" Hart snaps as he raises his hands. He turns his back on us.

Elixr repeats her damage statements. Hart gives a low hum. I shiver from the sense of his anger and frustration.

"I'm sorry."

He ignores my apology.

We step into onto the bridge and I gulp as I see the orb of the planet approaching rapidly in the window. Hart completely ignores me, and the view, as he focuses. He gives Elixr other commands with a firm authority. Long deccas pass as he works to bring the sublight navigation back online and gain some control of the ship.

I feel the Gs as we pull out of the uncontrolled spin and slam on the breaks. Even with the ship's inertial dampeners working, the sudden deceleration rocks the ship and it shudders as it slows.

Time feels like a swirl of chaos as long deccas seem to pass as rapidly as ticks.

"Fourteen deccas to impact," Elixr counts.

"We're going to crash?" Wish asks. She sounds so young. I pull her tight against me, clinging to my little sister as if I could save her from what is about to happen.

"We'll be okay. Hart can fix this." I glance at the planet as we loom ever closer. "You can fix it, can't you Hart?"

Beside us Hart swears. "Chortessa's guts! Pull up you lumbering lame bird."

"Thirteen deccas to impact."

Hart continues to fight the controls. The ship makes slow shifts but the planet continues to grow larger and larger. Elixr continues to count down the deccas of our approach. As we pass into the planet's atmosphere, the green shimmer of the ship's shields activate. Flames flicker along the edges of the shield. I hold my breath, hoping the haze clears while the shields last.

"Two deccas to impact."

Time feels like it slows down as the ground

comes into sight. The flames flicker away. We soar through the sky, plummeting toward the rock and stone in the distance.

"Brace for impact!" Elixr announces in her calm, unruffled voice.

The crunch of metal and glass impacting rock splinters through my ears and we're thrown forward, slamming into the wall. The clang of Hart's chromium head and body hitting the metal walls rings out and his hover drive stalls. He crumples to the floor but his head moves. His blue orbs are wide as if he's dazed. My head buzzes, spinning from the impact. In my arms, Wish whimpers.

Around us, the cheery voice of the ship tinkles. "We have reached our destination. Current Nar time in the capital is factor six twelve, on the seventh of Jarnoot, forty-seven fifty-six. Point five factors until sunrise.

Hart groans, reactivating his hover drive and pulling himself upright. With a wry grimace, as he rubs his spherical head, he says, "Welcome to Nar!"

8

Grounded

Tye

Ke-am gives a low growl at the dust cloud that pulses toward us. I lift my cloak, tucking my head beneath it as the dirt crashes over us like an epic wave from the Pliyoshi shorelines. We both shake off the dirt after the cloud passes.

"What in Chortessa's guts was that?" I say, gazing to the searing metal scrap as it continues to glide across the dirt toward us. I start to wonder if it might make sense to get out of the way but Ke-am is standing firm beneath me. He's watchful but calmly patient and I've learned to trust his instincts. The wreckage slows, coming to stop about four furlongs away.

It's some sort of ship, like a settlement transport but much larger. The metal exterior gleams red hot and sparks fly from a rear engine. She's a sweet looking ship and I calculate the value of the parts in my head. From what I can just see on the outer hull, I'd put it to an easy three orbits worth of staples. Maybe six if both of the ion thrusters are still functioning and supplied with xenon, and seven if there's an intact jump drive aboard.

"Let's check it out, Ke-am." The tiolf lifts his furry head and I scratch behind his left ear. He gives a low growl of pleasure, swishes his tail, and then stalks forward. There's no point approaching at speed, stealth is definitely the better option, because enough of that ship is intact that there could be survivors on board. The boat's worth nothing to me if its crew figures to kill me for trying to take it.

We circle around as we get closer because there's no telling what might be watching from the bridge. Ke-am lets out a low growl as lights flicker over the ship's hull. I stroke his fur, feeling the thick muscles of his shoulders beneath me. We've both got our gazes fixed on the old boat and Ke-am's step falters as he senses my shock when the ship's name comes into sight. It's painted in large letters on the hull.

"No!" I gasp, not sure I'm reading it correctly. "It can't be." I slide down from Ke-am's back and step toward the ship myself, not sure if I can believe what I'm seeing. Ke-am's giant head nudges up beside me. I reach out, absently stroking his muzzle. "No one back home will ever believe me if I tell 'em what we found, Ke-am." Ke-am gives a low growl as if asking me what I'm talking about.

"No one has heard hide nor hair of the Elixr in two hundred narcycles." Mamum told me about it when I was little but I always thought it was just some old children's bedtime story the Faithful took to heart. Now I wonder. I whistle low and then freeze as the lights in the shuttle bay flicker on and three figures move across the loading dock. A ledge glides out from the edge of the bay creating a rising platform.

Beside me, Ke-am growls and crouches low against the scrub of the Shadowlands beneath us. I drop to my belly and scramble forward to peer at them over the edge of the impact crater. My heart is racing as I watch the people. I reach behind me to pull my scope from my back satchel and fumble with the settings before lifting it to my eyes.

The droid is relatively small, only half the size of the two Narians, but since he's only half a body – a torso, arms, and head with no legs – he's probably a reasonable size up close. The Narian girl looks young, her body still not mature under the skin-tight body suit, although she's cute to look at. Her hair is this striking white blonde I've not seen outside of the Palace's Virreal harem and the historical paintings of the Bellamy royals. And she's so clean. Ain't no one so clean on all of Nar unless they're rich enough to never leave the City of Light. Just stepping into the Shadowlands leaves a trail of murk on your skin. You feel like you can't wipe it clean without a second moon's measure of bathing and none of the Faithful have the staples to afford that kind of luxury.

Beside her, the guy in the long coat has similar features. In fact, his face is so smooth and clean I shift uncomfortably, admiring his beauty, and then wonder at myself for the feeling. He stands tallest of the three. Similar white blonde hair but tied back and tucked beneath the collar of his coat. "What the?" I twist the zoom on my scope and gasp as the cut and markings of his full-length coat come into focus. "No! It can't be!"

No one's seen those colours, not in my lifetime, but everyone knows what they are. The face, the coat, the eyes are described in detail all over the catacombs. There's even a rough hewn statue in the main hub and every Book of Bellamy has his description on the back. The name on the ship, the markings on their clothes, the eerie familiarity of the stance and state of the guy, it all paints a picture of a legend that's been myth for generations.

For a long while, they gaze at the hull of the ship, walking its edges, but before they head back inside the tall one turns and scans the horizon. His eyes pass over Ke-am and me as if seeing into the black. I sink back against the dirt. He can't possibly see me. The Shadowlands have at least that going for them. We're lost in the murk. But that's when the real evidence flashes and a feeling, excitement, terror, or both, flutters through my gut. Those eyes that flash even in the darkness. Captain Bellamy's eyes. I lean close to Ke-am and whisper, "He's back!"

Niah

The horizon of this strange black world sends an eerie shiver down my spine. I can't help but feel like it's watching me, its shadows full of menace and judgement. It rises up along a crater's ridge around the ship. The barren dirt of the surface is washed in a heavy shadow of darkness. It sits upon us all and I can already feel it crawling over my skin.

I turn back to the ship and take a final walk around the edges to see what I can of her hull and exterior. She's not too banged up, thank goodness. The externals of the jump drive are mostly intact, although that doesn't solve the issue of the orkrane we'll need for the plasma conversion and dispersal of the cure. The sublights are a little more damaged. The right thruster lost its cathode neutraliser. I tap my tablet, running an internal diagnostic. "Eagrim's beak," I curse, glancing at the negative functions. Both the jump and sublight engines are offline.

Beside me, Hart is fussing. His ranting hasn't let up and I know he's furious, mostly at me. I still feel guilty as the nine-voids myself. "What were you thinking, you ignorant youngling? You could have killed us all. Who knows if Elixr will ever fly again? You may still have killed us all if we can't get her working. You may have killed all of Nar. You may have caused me to fail my mission, to fail my captain."

I sigh and let his words wash over me. I deserve them. "Look," I say when he finally pauses for a moment. "I'm pretty sure I can fix the ship. We might need some parts to get her flying again but given the readings of comparable air, water, and earth on this planet it would make sense that the mineral deposits we need for functional parts could be found here. It'll just take time."

"Time! Time! You're always talking about time. We may be too late already!" He looks around us and his eyes droop. He lets out a slow whine. "Oh Nar, have we failed you?"

Wish turns, snapping at him. "Shut up about it already, would you? She can't stop time, Hart. We're doing the best we can."

The robot huffs and glides away, back into the ship. It's almost a stalk, and the hover jet has tinges of purple in it which I suspect are a result of his stroppy anger. "I'll be in the lab running scans for deposits of ore then. And deposits of life. At least we can find out if there's anything left to save."

"Fine," I say, then take one last look at Elixr's hull. I stroke the still warm metal and sigh.

"It's not really your fault, Niah. Don't listen to him." Wish's words are kind but I know she's wrong.

"I was stupid, Wish. If I hadn't asked Elixr to fly silent she'd have had time to warn us about the impending collision. I completely forgot that Hart was still navigating when I powered him down. He looked like he was sleeping, you know?" I shake my head and walk back through the shuttle bay toward the lift. "Come on, we should check out the engine room and try to get the engines back online. We stressed the nine-voids out of the hydro thrusters trying to get her down safely."

She walks beside me, silent, and I think she can tell that I'm feeling sorry enough for myself as it is.

The engine room is covered in an odd blue mist, but there are no life support warnings so I assume it's just a minor xenon leak. I look over the equipment and sigh as I see the metal warping of the magnetic rings. "Damn, we're going to need more chromium to fix those."

I feel a sudden wave of dizziness and reach out to catch myself on the edge of the turbine. With my other hand I rub the pounding headache at my temples. I yawn and then rub the back of my neck. "Chortessa's guts I'm tired and sore. Must have been a harder landing than I thought."

Wish steps toward me clearly worried. "You okay, Niah? You don't look so good."

Pain stabs through my stomach and I retch. The blended contents of spirit water and ration bars create a sticky stain on the deck of the engine room. I groan, clutch my stomach, and crumple to my knees. "I don't feel so good." Around me the ship seems to sway. My ears ring and, even as I close my eyes, spots form behind my eyelids. I feel another rise of nausea. I retch again, dry this time.

"Niah!" Wish cries out as I fall to the floor. I try to open my eyes but they're so heavy. And everything is hot, so hot. My head feels like it's trying to explode.

"Wish? I–" I'm not even sure what I was going to say but I can't finish. Maybe just resting a little would help. I close my eyes and listen to Wish's frantic cries as she calls for help. I feel her arms around me but everything is too heavy. I'm too heavy to even stay awake.

Terror spikes within me when I realise that I'm falling asleep. I panic that I might not wake up again but even the adrenaline of fear doesn't give me the strength to force my eyes open. Instead, there's only blackness.

9

No Longer Alone

Wish

"Niah! Niah!" I cry, trying to wake her. She feels heavy, like a corpse in my arms, but I pull her back out of the room. "Elixr! Dammit, answer me!"

"How can I assist you Whiskey-One-Sierra-Four?"

"Niah's sick!"

"Records indicate that Ship Doctor Eric Samson has been deceased for approximately seventeen narcycles. There is no doctor in our current manifest."

"There's no doctor, Elixr. It's just us. Tell me how to fix her."

There's a pause as the ship seems to consider its options. "I am not fitted with telemetry tech capable of performing diagnostic scans or surgeries from this floor. Please deliver patient to the medical lab."

"Where in the nine-voids is the medical lab?" I remember seeing it but feel completely turned around trying to remember the way. A part of me is terrified that she's got the same sickness that caused Captain Bellamy to jettison his crew. If she did, it might be too late for Nar now. And too late for Niah, too.

I push the defeating thought to the fringes of my mind as lights blink up along a wall. I breathe a sigh of relief and haul Niah down the corridor. She's heavy but I feel amazing and strong and fast. My heart's pumping and I've never felt more alive, although, given that I've only been awake for a couple of circuits, I guess I don't have much to compare the feeling with. Maybe it's from the atmosphere of the planet strengthening my lungs or something in the blue haze of the engine room but I'm stronger and more capable than I've ever been. I haul Niah through the ship, following the directions on the wall, up two decks, and eventually find the medical lab.

I lift Niah up to the diagnostics pod. She looks so fresh and healthy and yet she was really, really sick before she passed out. I bite my lip and tuck her arms beside her then glance around for some sort of interface. "Elixr, how do I work this thing? Eagrim's beak, Niah would know what to do."

The holo lights up around her and I step back, startled. "Scanning, please wait." Elixr's voice is reassuring. I feel a bit silly letting it calm me because the ship's verbal response never shows emotion, so it's not like she would sound worried even if she could be, but it's good to know she knows what to do.

The lights of the holo move up and down Niah's

body and seem to take measures and graphs and blipping lines of diagnostics. A quarter factor passes as the program runs but Elixr remains silent. I step forward impatiently and rest my hands on the side of the bed, wishing I could reach in to hold Niah's hand. "Well?"

A series of charts blink into a column of text and images down one side of the holo. I see the bouncing line and beeping strokes of her heart rate ticks before the real thing starts pulsing into the room through the audio. I sigh with relief because, while I didn't think she was dead, it is really, really good to know she is alive.

"What's wrong with her?"

"Diagnostics indicate coma caused by hypertensive encephalopathy."

"What does that mean? How do we fix it?"

"Treatment, phlebotomy, haemoglobin reduction of two units recommended."

"Will that fix her?"

"Immediate response should restore consciousness and reduce symptoms."

"Then do it, do the haemoglobin thing. Save her!"

"Unable to facilitate extraction. Experienced medical staff unavailable."

"Of course there's no staff! All you've got is me! All she's got is me." I'm frantic, gripping her hand and wishing I knew more about anything at all that would help her. "Please, Elixr, tell me what to do!"

I sigh in relief as she starts listing what I need to set up. I rummage through the drawers, hunting for needles and tube and bags and everything. Thank goodness the medical unit is well organised.

Everything's sterile and I realise I'm probably not, so I swab my hands with several of the alcohol wipes and then feel guilty because they're probably a limited resource on this tub. I shrug it off because all that matters right now is Niah and getting her to wake up again.

I fit together the pieces exactly as Elixr describes. She walks me through each step and I give thanks again that her voice is calm, methodical, and completely in control. I practically collapse on top of Niah when I finally see the draw of red blood travelling through the tube. I pull a stool up beside the diagnostic pod and watch as the bag slowly begins to fill.

Hart finds me like that. Eyes fixed on Niah, waiting for her to wake up. Willing her to.

"You must complete her mission," Hart says as he comes into the room.

I glance up at him and I know my mouth is fixed in a stubborn line because I'm still angry at the way he's making all this Niah's fault. "Go away!"

He hums, then glides forward. "This was always a potential outcome. You must complete her mission."

"Don't you see, she's sick! She might be dying."

"She has always been dying. That is why you exist."

I blink at him not sure I heard him correctly and not sure I really want to know what he's talking about. But I can't not ask. I can't not know. "What do you mean?"

Hart looks down on Niah. His blue orb eyes seem almost gentle as they gaze on her and I can't help but feel maybe he does care about her a little. I guess he's watched over us both for narcycles, our whole lives, in his own way.

"Before your creation, we detected a genetic defect in her DNA. Her condition is degenerative and terminal. Sensing that she might not live to complete Captain Bellamy's final instructions, we created a second clone from an alternative source."

"Terminal?" The word seems to buzz in my ears. "You mean she'll die?"

Hart's chassis lifts in a shrug. "There are treatments that will prolong her but in her first narcycles we monitored her vital statistics carefully. It is clear that her particular case of Polycythemia vera is acute and degenerative. We have attempted to carefully control her environment on the ship to minimise overstimulation of her red blood cell production and administered Pegylated interferon to limit further damage, but even in optimal conditions there is strain on her body. Exposure to the airborne xenon in the engine room hyper-stimulated her condition. It is only a matter of time before her organs are irreparably damaged and begin to systematically fail."

I suddenly wish Hart's voice was as emotionless as Elixr's because the solemnity of his voice drives home the truth of every word. I shake my head, not wanting to believe it. "Why didn't you tell us? We would have been more careful. We could have kept her sleeping!"

"A fault in my system memories prevented me from accessing vital parts of my archives until my recent reboot. Now I remember."

I swipe at the tears streaming down my cheeks. I suck a breath through my nose, drawing back the snot, then swipe at that too with the sleeve of my suit.

"We must acquire the necessary components to complete the mission," Hart says. I bite my lip and rest my head against the soft material of Niah's coat.

"I don't want to hear it. Just go away."

"You must fulfil your purpose. It is your reason for being."

I lift my head, turning my gaze on him, angry as the nine-voids. "Don't tell me what my life is worth! Chortessa's guts, I'll rip your circuits out of your arse and feed your parts to the fabricator."

Hart's small blue eyes blink and he tilts his head. "Your emotional response is not computable."

"Don't you get it? My sister is dying! Just leave me alone. I need to be with her."

"But the mission—"

"To all the nine-voids! The baull-scat mission can wait! I won't leave her until she wakes up. I won't leave her alone when she's sleeping. She needs me to be here."

Hart gazes at me for a long moment but I ignore him. Eventually, he lets out a weak hiss, like a sigh, and glides to the door. "We will wait until November-One-Alpha-Four wakes. The ore extraction may require more effort than just your own. But our mission cannot wait forever. It has waited long enough."

He sighs again when I refuse to look at him or

answer. Right now, I just don't give an eagrim's beak about his mission or about Nar. Right now, all that matters is Niah.

Niah

My heart races as I feel the darkness around me but begins to slow when I open my eyes. I am awake. Everything will be fine. I lift a hand to my head. My temples still throb. Nausea swirls in my stomach. I groan. "What happened?"

Beside me, Wish lets out a breath and clutches my fingers. "Niah," she whispers. Tears stream down her face. I try to push myself up, to find out what's wrong, but she puts a hand on my shoulder to hold me in place. It feels easier not to move anyway so I lay there and just gaze at her.

"What's going on, Wish?"

She swallows. "You got sick. But you're okay now." Her voice hitches at the end so I know she's lying but I don't want to dig any deeper right now.

"If I'm fine, then I can sit up, right?"

Wish glances at the door and I realise Hart is pacing there.

"She's still too weak, Hart. We need more time."

"Every moment we waste our planet is dying."

"Niah's–" Wish's voice fades away and I wonder what she didn't want to say.

"What, Wish?"

She shakes her head. Hart's hover engine hums as he spins in place and then travels toward the medical pod. "We must complete the mission. While there is still time."

"What are you saying?"

"Don't tell her, Hart."

"Tell me, Hart." The droid makes a grinding noise and I'm not sure if it's supposed to represent frustration, like someone grinding their teeth, or confusion, like the grinding cogs of a brain that can't decide the best course of action. Growing more and more frustrated at their secrets I say again, my voice quiet but firm, commanding, Bellamy. "Tell me, Hart."

His blue orbs blink and he dips his head. "You have a mutation of the Janus kinase-2 gene which, in your case, led to a fatal flaw in your genetic construction. Your condition is degenerative, meaning your symptoms will worsen over time. We must complete the mission before it is too late."

I pause, wondering if the words are making any sense. "I'm dying?" I whisper. Inside, a part of me already dreads that endless sleep, another part seems to have always anticipated it, always known. And yet in the moment of silence between all of us I still hope they'll tell me I misunderstood, that I'm fine, that everything is going to be okay.

"Your condition is terminal." Hart's voice is blunt but not emotionless and, in a way, that's harder because he seems to care. "It's factor seven, and you are recovered enough that we should begin orkrane extraction immediately."

"She's not ready!" Wish shouts at the droid. I close my eyes both against the pain of the truth sinking into my heart and the volume of her voice, the violence of her anger.

I take a breath, open my eyes again, then reach

out a hand to Wish. "It's okay. We need to do this. We were meant to do this, Wish. It's our reason for being."

"Who gives an eagrim's beak what they want from us, Niah? What right do they have to dictate the fate of our lives? I don't care that we were made from someone else's genetic material, or even that we're supposed to be some second coming created to save an entire world. This is your life–my life– they can't just decide the value of it. It doesn't work that way. YOU get to choose. You, Niah."

I bite my lip and turn to really look at her. I wait for her to meet my gaze. Her cool blue eyes are washed with tears. They soften as if deep inside, her heart is already broken, already mourning me. And maybe that hurts the most but I can't let it, so I tell her what I'm supposed to tell her. "I get this circuit. We get this circuit, Wish. Because we were meant for this. And we get to do something big, something no one else can do, something Bellamy, the crew, all gave their lives for. We get to save everyone else."

Wish stares at me a long moment and I force myself not to fall apart in front of her. I force myself to believe every word of what I've said even though inside I'm furious and just want to curl up and forget the world, forget that any of it exists at all. Her head tips and her whole body shudders as she leans against me. I stroke a hand through her hair and wait the long deccas until her breathing becomes more even.

She finally looks back up at me and nods. "Yeah," she says, then sighs as if she's letting grace and faith take us. "Okay then. Let's do this."

10

The Shadowland

Niah

Outside, the sky is still as black as coal and filled with a murk that sticks to our skin as we move. Despite the darkness, the air is increasingly scorching with a drenching humidity that makes it hard to breathe.

Wish hooks up a transport tray to a mini-zip. I eye the death trap of chromium and glass with its own small hydro thruster and hover-jets. She straddles it, leaning forward over the handlebars as it shimmies down the platform to the surface of the planet. She reaches a hand behind her and taps on the seat. "Are we doing this?"

I glance at Hart. He mounts himself on a grid of the transport tray beside the drill platform. The transport beam locks him into place.

I swallow, nod, then swing my leg over the back of the mini-zip and clutch Wish's waist as she revs the engine. I put my feet on the pedals and we roar off. The wind whips my face and murky air fills my lungs. I tip my face down against Wish's back and just hold on tight. Zip-gliding was never my thing. Which is an odd thing to think because I've obviously never done it before, so I imagine the feeling is a remnant from the genetic memories of Bellamy.

A beam of light splits the darkness in front of us and Wish uses it to guide the mini-zip through the dunes and crevices of the shadowed lands beyond the lights of the ship. A map overlay displays the blinking sources of orkrane, guiding her.

We've travelled barely a furlong when, from the corner of my eye, I glimpse a slinking shape. Its form is just visible in the outer edges of the light. My jaw drops as I realise it's a boy riding a giant tiolf. I tap Wish on the shoulder and she glances at the boy, then draws up the mini-zip. We gaze at him together.

The boy and his creature ride toward us. His chin is lifted and his broad shoulders are back, but his whole body flows with the movement of the animal beneath him. It's almost as if boy and beast are one. The slinky striped fur of the animal is smudged with dirt, and so is the boy. They look wild, and wilder still to imagine that the boy must have tamed a beast notorious for its unbreakable spirit. As we watch, the animal tilts back its head. Its howl echoes from the dunes around us.

"Am I seeing things?" I whisper to Wish.

She shakes her head. "If you are, then I am too. Is that boy riding a tiolf?"

"Looks like it."

I hold my breath as they come closer. The air

around us is still and silent. The boy raises a hand as if in greeting and I start to mirror his action, then startle and reach my hands to cover my ears as a screeching alert sounds from behind us. Lights flash on the ship and a siren blares over and over again. In an instant, the animal, boy clinging to its back, bounds away and pelts off in the opposite direction. They disappear from sight in ticks.

I spin around, glaring at the ship and the droid behind me. "What in Chortessa's guts, Hart?"

The alert dies down and the lights return to normal as the droid splutters with a startled beep.

"What was that?" Wish asks.

"Elixr reports that the xenon has reached critical levels in the ion thruster reserves."

"All that noise was because the ion thrusters are out of juice?"

He nods. "It's a critical system. After your episode in the engine room, I scheduled a subroutine to filter the xenon into secondary storage until the thrusters can be repaired."

"Okay," I say, "so we still have plenty of xenon. We'll get the ion thrusters back up and running eventually. Right now we're getting orkrane so we can dispense the cure. Let's go."

I wrap my arms around Wish again and she jets the engines into gear. We zip off toward the nearest deposit which is several furlongs south. I watch for life signs on my tablet as we glide through the rise and fall of the land around us. On the screen I can see the boy and tiolf continue heading farther and farther away. Eventually, they disappear from the edge of the scanner's range. There are other lifeforms in the distance too, but nothing heading toward us and no immediate danger or threat.

It's eerie zipping through the shadows. Rising up out of the murk and dirt are glimpses of what Nar must have been before. Light from the mini-zip hits the edges of derelict buildings that reach up into the sky. At one point we glide through a forest of damaged and destroyed solar arrays. They rise out of the ground like trees, searching for twin solars they can no longer find through the murk.

When we reach the orkrane deposit, the three of us position the drill platform. As chunks of ore are drawn up from beneath the surface of the planet, we haul the chunks up onto the tray. They get caught up in the transport beams. I set the system to defabricate the ore and each large chunk is broken down into its molecular structure and stored in ticks.

Even with the advanced tech in the drilling platform, it takes a quite a few factors to extract enough ore. Eventually, we have enough raw material based on the calculations I ran for the correct ratio of plasma conduction.

Wish leans back against the transport tray as the drill winds down with a final spinning hum. She wipes a hand across her forehead which is now filthy, not just with the dark murk of these lands but the black ink of the orkrane ore.

"Job's done?" She asks.

I smile at her and nod my head. "Now to get it all back to the ship and get this party started."

We mount up and begin heading back toward the ship.

"Wait," Wish calls back to me. Her voice is almost whipped away in the wind as the mini-zip glides along.

"What is it?" I shout back.

She pulls up and I lean over her shoulder as she points to the holo-display. "I think there's a settlement over there." She points to a cluster of lifeforms that pulse with energy. There's dozens of them.

I bite my lip. "It could be a nest of eagrims for all we know."

"We should check it out. The boy had to come from someplace and if there are people there they might be willing to help us fix Elixr. We need more hands to extract enough chromium to do all the repairs she needs. Maybe they would trade with us?"

She's right, but I feel a nervous tension about approaching populated areas. "You're right." I sigh and nod. "Okay, let's go check it out."

We zip over the dunes, heading closer to the blur of lifeforms on the tablet. Beneath us, the ground whizzes by so fast that I wonder how Wish can see to keep us on solid ground. The furlongs pass beneath us but there are still several to cover before we reach the settlement. Even so, as we get closer, we see a wall of orbs rising up out of the blackness. Light shines off their metallic surfaces. Above each, long rods spear upward to the sky. Beneath, long columns thrust into the ground below. I watch with awe as we move closer and closer.

Wish lifts her head, thrusting her chin at the display. I gaze over her shoulder at it to see what she's indicating. With a finger she points at the small blurry dot that's keeping pace alongside us. Because of the cargo, the transport tray attached to our rear, and the pitch black of the land around us, we're not moving at anything like the mini-zip's top speed so it's not impossible for a wild animal to be keeping pace. But even so, it's a sight to see and something very much to be wary of.

Wish and I glance in that direction but I see nothing but the blinding ink of the shadows around us. Suddenly the mini-zip stalls out. Its engines splutter, flicker, and then fade to black. Around us, the darkness is complete.

"Chortessa's guts!" Wish swears. I feel the muscles in her shoulders clench as she uses all her strength to control the mini-zip beneath us. It slams into the dirt hard, sending a scatter of stone, rock, and earth flying in all directions. We're both thrown forward and my weight propels hers through the air. Together, we crash hard against the ground which gives way beneath us. We tumble, falling.

I reach out to grasp the crumbling soil in my hands. I scramble as the walls of dirt rise up around us but can't stop myself falling. We slam into the hard-packed earth at the bottom of the pit. My breath bursts from my lungs. I lay stunned as a flurry of grit tumbles down over us.

Beside me, Wish splutters, coughing back the dust.

Then, over our heads, we hear a heavy crunch of metal and a whirling whizz and plink. I lift my hands up to cover my face and curl myself into as small a ball as possible as the hunk of chromium slams into the dirt walls above us, bouncing back and forth slightly before landing in a heap just inches from my head.

"Ouch!" Hart says, his blue orbs blinking as if he's stunned.

"What are you talking about you hunk of scrap? You didn't feel a thing. You're made of metal." Wish pushes herself upright with a groan.

Hart blinks at her. "I have been programmed with empathic sensors that can anticipate painful events and replicate the appropriate response."

"Anticipate? You didn't anticipate us getting thrown from the mini-zip. THAT would have been helpful."

I lay back and close my eyes, wishing my head would stop spinning and that they would stop shouting.

Beside me, Wish thumps against the high dirt walls of the pit. "Eagrim's beak. I think we're stuck in here. How are we going to get out?" I cough, feeling the ache through every inch of my body. Wish kneels down beside me. "Niah, you okay?"

I nod but it's probably not very convincing. "I'll live." I glance up above us and feel an odd comfort to see light. It creates a soft haze through the shadows of murk. I feel less comfort when I realise it's the steaming hunk of mini-zip which ultimately put us in this predicament. It rests just inches from the drop above our heads.

I groan as I sit up. In the dark pit, Hart's hover stream creates a soft glow of blue light. That and his eyes serve as a means of illumination in our little hole.

"We appear to be in a predicament." The droid states. I can't help but laugh at the understatement of it all. Then cough at the dirt in the air.

Wish sighs. "How are we going to get out of this mess?"

11

Not Exactly A Warm Welcome

Tye

I dig in at the outskirts of the line of light that creates a border between the Shadowland and the Outer Rim. From this vantage point I can make out the dark pit where the strangers landed when they were thrown in the crash. Their smoked out mini-zip sits in a steaming heap several feet away, which is probably lucky because if it had kept grinding through the dirt it might have landed on top of them.

Beside me, Ke-am gives a low growl and drags along on his belly. I reach over and stroke his fur. "Easy, boy." He's impatient too. We both want to go down there and get a closer look but it's not a good idea. The Stalkers are never far from their traps and as much as they might turn a blind eye to my illegal salvage in the Shadowlands, they wouldn't take kindly to my getting into affairs with aliens. And having any association with one that looks like him is quite probably a death sentence.

Rebecca Laffar-Smith

I hang back and wait. Before long, a hulking mamot lumbers over the rise. Its giant head sways as it walks with clomping feet that kick up dust with every step. Its claws dig grooves into the earth. On her back, a troop of six Stalkers sit astride the mamot's carrier platform. They're dressed in black shadow cloaks and blend perfectly with the murky earth of the Shadowland and the equally dark leathery skin of the mamot.

As they near the hole in the ground, one traces down one of the mamot's large horns. With an agile step he jumps to the ground. He throws back his hood and beams a light into the pit. I recognise him, Hanzor. He's a nice enough guy but arrogant, greedy, and he doesn't like surprises.

"Ho there!" he calls and I wonder if the aliens speak our language enough to understand him.

There's a muffled response from the hole but I can't make it out. Hanzor laughs which makes me all the more curious about what they said. I scramble closer. It's risky because I'm now in the light cast by the nearest Outer Rim tower sphere, but my own shadow cloak blends with the rock and I'm covered in enough murk at the best of times that I'm betting to odds they won't see me.

Beside me Ke-am whines and goes to shimmy alongside me but I wave him back. A little moon-skitter like me can go unnoticed but even covered in murk and dirt Ke-am's size stands out against the dunes. He whines again but keeps his place, gazing after me as I continue to crawl away. I keep to the dunes so the rise of my body over the dirt won't stand out.

"You got a mouth on ya, don't you little moon-skitter?" Hanzor calls down the hole. "Better watch it else I decide to roast it from your face." With a grin, he levels a plasma pulser, pointing it down into the hole. The weapon's searing white glow gleams in the darkness.

"Let us out of here you ugly baull-scat!" the girl's voice calls back up to him.

"Wish!" hisses another voice, reprimanding the girl. It's soft and feminine, too, so I can't figure out which of the three must have spoken. Could their droid have a feminine voice unit?

"Watch your tongue, void-scum. I ain't above cutting it out of you." Hanzor turns to his crew who are scrambling down from the back of the carrier beast. "Haul them up and make sure you secure them with zap-links. We don't want them running off or crying out for help."

They haul out the robot first. I still can't get a great look at it. It seems to be cooperative and calm. I wonder if it's programmed for defence or if its subroutines prevent it acting against a Narian command.

The girl comes up next and she's far less cooperative. She yanks against the three guys gripping her arms. The hood falls off the guy at her back and the white rims of his eyes stand out against his dark skin. I know him as Erron. "Stop wriggling ya void-scum." He levels a plasma pulser at her hip and digs in slightly.

She twists her head to glare at him. "Make me!" Erron's white teeth gleam in the low light and he yanks her hair. She winces and I imagine she's feeling the ache because they're not being gentle despite her having so slight a figure. A third man grips her wrists between his fingers and then slams a zap-link over them before shoving her forward. She slams against the ground and huffs out a breath before turning back to the men. Her crystal-ice eyes gleam, flashing with anger. She spits at them.

They haul up the last figure from the trap and my breath catches as I see the coat, the hair, the face, the eyes. The men's hands fall away as they finally seem to see it too.

"Eagrim's beak!" Hanzor gasps, stepping back.

"Niah, run!" the girl shouts. She pushes herself to her feet and begins scrambling away but her friend seems frozen in the stunned gazes of their captors.

Two of the six men drop to their knees. Against the dirt their breath fluffs up clouds of murk as they mutter.

"Bellamy."

"He's returned!"

"It's Bellamy."

Hanzor grimaces, and triggers a master control. Several dozen volts rip through the zap-links around the girl's wrists and she convulses as the electricity pulses through her. Those things deliver a hurt so hard you wish for a tick that they had floated you in the nine-voids instead, but they don't cause any lasting damage. Still, the girl seems much more subdued and lays motionless against the dirt after the convulsions stop.

Hanzor reaches down and yanks up the Stalker nearest him. "Cut it out you ignorant murk-scum.

Of course it isn't the Captain. That legend is two hundred narcycles old! Does this moon-skitter look two hundred narcycles to you?"

The man looks unsure but Hanzor steps forward and grabs the collar of the Captain's coat. He leans in close to glare into those penetrating, eerie eyes. "You're..." he shakes his head. "No, you can't be him." His voice fades away and he swallows. "But, you're near enough to fake it. Certainly enough to keep Thomis happy. Come on, guys! This haul is going to mint us enough staples to live in the Inner Circle for a hundred circuits. Take him!"

Still uncertain, the other men hesitate, but with Hanzor's grip soon joined by Erron's and another of their companions, the other men soon fall into line. They snap a zap-link around Bellamy's wrists, haul all three captors up onto the carrier platform of their mamot, and head in the direction of the nearest Outer Rim tower.

Niah

"Chortessa's guts!" I whisper. I wonder that I can't come up with a more apt expression of the predicament we are in but I still don't know exactly how screwed we are.

"Not the friendliest of welcomes," Hart states in his bland, understated way.

"You think? These baull-scat void-scum better not lay another volt on me or I'm going to rip their teeth out through their noses and shove them up their–"

"Wish," I say, trying to stem her tirade before she

gets any more worked up. I lift my hands to my aching head. They're bound before me so I don't have full range of motion but at least I can press a thumb into the throbbing pain between my eyes.

Wish glances at me, concerned. "You okay?" She shuffles forward, her hands still bound behind her by the zap-links.

I'm so wiped out that I just want to sleep but I don't want to close my eyes. Not in this place, usually not ever, but I know I can't stay awake forever. The swaying lumber of the mamot beneath us is almost relaxing except for the fact that I don't feel entirely secure at this height. Even with the six men surrounding us, it seems precarious to let my guard down.

"I'm okay. I just don't know what's going on."

The guy nearest us leans close to whisper but I imagine his commander can still hear him. "You're him, ain't ye? They always said he'd come back. We been waiting and watching so long."

I swallow because I'm already dreading what I think this guy believes. "I don't know what you mean."

"I became a Stalker because I believed in ye. Ever since I was a boy. Nothing but a moon-skitter myself, maybe even younger than her." He lifted his chin to indicate Wish. "But I believed ye would be back. And I believed I'd be the one to find ye."

"Erron, shut your trap," the man guiding the mamot by a heavy set of reigns snarls. The Narian beside us hunches his shoulders, sits back, and falls silent. But his eyes remain fixed on me. In fact, five sets of eyes cling so tightly to my back and face that my skin crawls and I wish I could detach from it and step out of myself.

"I'm not what you think."

As we get closer and closer to the giant glowing sphere, more and more light casts out across us. The men haul us down from the mamot. The commander unclicks the zap-links from my wrists and tucks them into his pocket. He lifts his plasma pulser to show he's still well armed and holds a grip on my arm so tight that I don't have the strength to pull away even if I truly had the energy. Together, we march through the entry at the foot of the tower, up the lifter platform, and into a busy room.

Silence falls around us as we enter but the commander ignores the rising whispers around us and marches through. His grip on my arm tightens but instead of wincing I lift my chin. From the outside, I imagine it looks like he's gently guiding me through the weave of people, so it's no wonder that rather than stepping forward to intercede, people are dropping to their knees.

I cringe as, one after another, people seem to see in me the face of their long-awaited saviour. A hum of prayer, whispers of wonder, and a flow of people gesturing and prostrating surrounds us.

An elderly man at the edge of the crowd cries out. "Bellamy! Bellamy you have returned to save us!" His cry echoes around the room above the hum of the whispering voices. I flinch at the thud of a plasma pulser cracking the man across the head. He grunts, crumpling to the floor in a whimper. The guard standing over him kicks him

111

in the gut with a heavy boot and he falls silent.

The crowd seems torn between hovering close and scattering away, afraid of further rebuke from the Stalkers. A brave old woman shuffles toward us, her hands outstretched. Beside me the commander snarls. With a nod of his head two of his men rush her, pulling her aside. I glance at him but he's hiding his displeasure behind a mask of open pride. I shake my head, disgusted at it all. "You know I'm not him. Why don't you say something!" I hiss.

"What, and lower your value? No way in the nine-voids. If they want to worship a ghost then let them. They can tear you to shreds for the fallacy after I've collected my staples."

He guides us through the maze of people and down another corridor. The rooms are oddly shaped, perhaps because they're housed within a giant column of spheres, or because they are mostly cobbled together from old scraps of tech that don't look like they have seen a maintenance technician in generations.

The people around us seem to become less populous the further through the sphere we travel and eventually, we pass only a handful of well-armed men. The tech becomes more derelict and dirty. Eventually, the commander pulls me up beside a gritty dark room. At the far edge, its window gazes out on the blackness of night but is secure behind thick layers of tempered glass. He thrusts me forward and I stumble into the room. The men behind him unlock the zap-links on Wish and Hart, then give them both similar shoves. We all turn to the door where they stand guarding the only exit.

"Right, keep the noise down, and don't bother trying to hack the door, droid. Its controls aren't electronic, they're mechanical. You need a key." He waves a chunky old key like the kind that was used before tech and snickers as he slams the door closed. I hear the heavy lock clink with a finality that makes me feel truly trapped for the first time since our capture.

After the men are gone, we spend a short while walking the walls of the enclosure trying to find a way out but there is nothing. Every inch of the place is made of cold iron. I feel the chill of it as I sit down.

I lean my back against the smooth curve of the outer wall and tip my head to gaze out of the window at the scatter of stars. From here, they're not so obscured by the murk and are almost pretty to look at in that strange, longing for a home among them, kind of way.

"I'm sorry, Niah. I should have been watching where we were going," Wish whispers. She sits beside me. She's stiff, as if she's trying to keep as much of her body from touching the cold surfaces of the floor and walls as possible. Even so, her little body shivers in the chill. I shrug out of my coat and wrap it around her shoulders. She tucks her arms in, sinking into it with a sigh. "What about you?"

I smile. "One advantage of my condition is that I run hotter than normal I guess." I shrug. "You need the warmth more than I do."

She sighs. "Thanks, Niah." Wish lifts a hand to

smother her yawn.

I reach out and draw her to me. "Come on, get some sleep. I suspect we're stuck here at least until someone comes to see us in the morning. The commander might want his bounty but, with the way people reacted outside, I don't think they mean to keep us prisoner, not forever."

"What if they do?"

"Then we'll figure it out. But for now, get some rest." She nods, and I settle her head on my knee. I run my fingers through her hair and before long her breath is smooth and even. I glance at Hart. "What about you?"

His orbs gaze at me and I feel like he's sad but who can tell what a droid is feeling? "I should conserve power." I nod, and then sigh as his hover-jets power down and he comes to rest. Even the orbs of his eyes blink out. Around me the silence is eerie.

I sit for a long while, not wanting to sleep, but I can't keep my eyes open. Fear runs through me. It drains me. Eventually, I give in and close my eyes, letting the exhaustion take me. Inside, as dreams start to flood my mind, I cling to the hope that I'll wake when the sun rises.

12

The City of Light

Niah

In the moments before really coming awake, my heart starts racing as if it senses danger. I thrash at the shadows behind my eyes. My hands slam against the cold iron floor and wall of the cell. Startled, I blink, open my eyes, and glance around at the soft lit room.

Not far from where I slept, Hart still lays dormant and dark. The chill of the cell seems cooler than I remember. I glance down at where Wish had been when I had closed my eyes. She isn't there.

"Wish?" I cry, glancing up. I peer into every shadow of the cell. "Wish!"

She's not here.

I push up from the wall and stalk around, searching, but there are only a handful of feet from wall to wall and door to window. It's not like there is anywhere she could hide. "Wish! Where are you?"

When she doesn't reply I lean against the iron

bars and shout into the hall beyond. "Wish! Where is my sister?"

The guards grunt a muttered, "Shu'p!"

"Chortessa's guts you baull-scat void-scum! Where in the nine-voids is my sister? You bring her back, you hear? Bring her back, right now!"

I reach over to Hart, shaking him. When he doesn't power up, I trigger his reset. He blusters slightly, his eye orbs flickering until a stream of text starts scrolling down his face. The lines of code don't make much sense.

"Hart?" He doesn't respond. His hover-jets remain silent and the text just scrolls over his screen in a loop. "Hart! Wake up you cross-wired bolt trap. We have to find Wish."

I turn, searching the cell for its weakest point. The door is secure, and leads to the greater danger of the well-armed guards. The walls are solid and probably lead to neighbouring cells. But light streams through the window, casting back the darkness. I lean close to the glass and realise it sits bedded in the warped and rusting metal of the structure.

"Maybe," I whisper, leaning against a piece of the metal. It gives, just barely, but enough to know that with time and effort I could probably unseat the glass panel enough for us to fit through. I dig into Hart's chest cavity which is mostly a cavern of wires, switches, and ports. But hidden deep is the rotor tool used to perform routine maintenance. I pull it free and use it to jimmy at the joins between the glass and the metal of the cell window. It makes a mild scratching noise and I glance back at the door, wondering if it will alert the guards.

By now, however, Hart's odd bootup sequence is causing him to make some strange noises of his own. With any luck, the guards will assume the droid is just blustering like the emotional wreck he is rather than effecting any kind of rescue or escape. I keep grinding at the join of glass and metal. Behind me, the robot continues to get louder and more disruptive. Eventually an alarm beeps from him in staccato bursts of ear-splitting pitch.

As the lock jangles on the cell door I shove the rotor-tool up the sleeve of my sleeper suit and turn to watch it open. A large, surly Stalker glares at the droid. In his hand, he holds a tray of food. "Shut that rust bucket up, would you?"

I shake my head and hold up my empty hands. "I don't know what's wrong with him. What did you do to him when you took my sister away?"

"Don't know what you're talking about, moon-skitter."

"My sister! She was with us. Where have you taken her?"

He raises an eyebrow. "You mean the guy in the coat? Bellamy? He's been taken before the Lord, he has. I 'magine the good ol' Lord of Light has some questions for him."

I feel a queasy swell in my stomach and bite back my tongue. I force myself to swallow before speaking. "You took the wrong person! She's not Bellamy. We've been trying to tell you people. This is all just one big mistake. You have to let us go."

The guard shakes his head and bends low, laying the tray on the floor. With a foot he sends the tray sliding across the distance between us. "Here, better eat up, last meal and all." He laughs, then turns and marches out through the door. He slams it closed and I shudder at the sound of heavy iron clanking into place. I glare at the food, push the tray aside, and turn back to the window. I'm going to get Wish back myself, even if I have to tear through all of Nar to find her.

I spend what is probably a factor digging away at the groove between metal and glass. My hands feel raw. All this effort and I've hardly made a gap. I grimace and drop my forehead against the window. This is never going to work. "Wish," I whisper, and gaze out through the glass.

From a distance, the settlement looks like a giant dome surrounded by a series of raised spheres. The spheres track a line along the outer rim between darkness and light. We're probably half a furlong off the ground. My eyes blur, either with tears or with trying to gaze into the distance.

Suddenly, a face pops into view. I stumble back, startled. I trip over my own feet, landing hard against the metal floor. The rotor tool falls from my hand and clangs on the ground beside me.

"Eagrim's beak! What was that?"

Wish

My cheek throbs and I lift my hand to it as my eyes adjust to the dim light. I remember pain. I remember rough hands gripping me. I remember thick, meaty fingers covering my mouth when I tried to scream. When I bit down on my captor's hand it snapped back, slamming into the side of my face so hard that I must have passed out. I lift my head, cautiously. Then move to sit up inside the small carriage.

"Woah, big fella," says a large man wearing a dark hooded cloak of rough animal hide. His hand clenches on my shoulder, shoving me back. His dark skin and white eyes cast sharp contrast.

"Let me up. I'm fine." The hand eases, but doesn't lift. I move more carefully, pushing myself upright until I'm leaning back against the cushioned seat. When it's clear I'm stable the hand falls away. "Where am I? Where are Niah and Hart?"

"Quiet, Bellamy."

Bellamy? He thinks… oh. It all begins to make sense now. They thought Niah was Bellamy, too. It must be her coat. I finger the lines on the sleeves, feeling the material heavy around me.

"Will you at least tell me where we are going?" I ask.

The guy watches me a long decca and I try not to squirm under his gaze. What would Niah do? Would she pretend to be Bellamy? Remembering the way his calm, haunted face stared down the lens of the holo-projector, I fix the guard with that same detached stare. He swallows, then says, "You're on your way to the Palace, Captain. Lord Oliver wants to be talking with you."

I furrow my brow, trying to work out the edges of the almost-familiar name. "Oliver?" It reminds me of hints of a childhood I never had.

"That's right, Captain. He wants to be having words."

119

I blink back the haze still lingering in my eyes. Around me, the dark walls of the carriage sway. I glance out the glass windows and blink in surprise to see streets lined in light and tall buildings. Everything seems crisp, and clean, and new.

"Where are we?"

The man blinks as if I'm both daft and stupid. Then a light dawns in his eyes and he nods. "Oh, right! I guess you ain't never seen the city. Left before the Lord created it. We're in the city. The great Lord's City of Light, that is. The only civilised place there is left on all of Nar."

I bite my lip, feeling like that's probably something significant, but even in my before memories I can't find a sense of what existed in the past. Instead, I gaze out at the strange, pale beauty of it all. Columns rise up, soaring into the sky. A zip-liner skims past on a hover rail overhead. Giant holo-screen billboards flash with the latest drinks or snacks or furnishings. Buildings of white, gold, and silver stand tall along the streets. And high beyond the reach of the tallest spires, a wash of midnight blue with wisps of white foam, a sprinkle of starlight, and the glow of three pale moons arch above us. A sky.

As we continue to weave our way through the traffic, I feel the awe of the place filling me. I lean my head against the glass, eyes fixed on the strange wonder outside. "Wow!" I sigh.

Across from me the guard grins. "Yep, she's something. Ain't she?"

I lift an eyebrow. "Yep, she's something."

In the maze of all this, how on Nar will I find

Niah, or will Niah find me?

13

If Only We Had Wings

Tye

I grit my teeth as I cling to the ledge on the tower sphere. The metal has a cool chill to it. It absorbs the sunless nights of the Shadowlands rather than the artificial suns in the City of Light. When her face appears in the glass, I nearly lose my grip on the ledge.

I wonder for a moment if I've climbed the wrong tower but it's not every circuit a Stalker hauls in an otherworld catch, and she looks too much like the young girl to be unrelated. But this is no Bellamy; it's no little girl, either. She is beautiful, with a shock of white-blonde hair so clean she can't have spent more than a circuit in the murk. Her face is free of lines as if she's never squinted at catacomb ash or the harshness of the City of Light's twin solars. Who is she?

She seems equally surprised to see me but I figure it's probably due to the half furlong between me and the void of darkness below. Tannan had said only a mind-sapped moon-skitter like myself would be fool enough to climb it. I glance at Jenin and Blake, who were fool enough to climb up here with me.

Jenin rubs the fingers of one hand down her thigh. "Eagrim's beak, my hands are like ice, Tye. I don't know how I let you talk me into this kind of crazy."

"At least I didn't ask you to ride an eagrim to get up here, Jenin." I grin at her because we both know that no one has managed to tame an eagrim yet. If anyone could it would be her. She laughs like she knows it.

"You daring me?"

Blake leans over. "Here." He holds out a pair of fingerless chortessa gloves. The soft fur is sure to warm Jenin's hands and ward off the chill. She smiles in gratitude and it's the kind of smile that stops a guy's heart. I look away, glad that the bitter wind prevents a flush from rising to my cheeks. It's none of my business what those two share but it still feels kind of weird to be a third wheel around them.

My gaze is captured again by the soft curves of the girl in the glass. Her eyes are fixed on me and she's mouthing something I can't hear. I point to my ear and shake my head to let her know I can't hear a word of what she's saying.

"How are we going to do this Tye?" Blake asks. He waves a hand at the glass. "The fitting is pretty solid. That's bound to be tempered glass so you can't expect to break it."

I shake my head.

"No, here." I wedge my leg against the rim of the building so that I can free up both arms. It feels pretty solid and secure to sit into the grooves of the structure like this but a breath hisses from between Jenin's teeth when I let go of the ledge and reach over my shoulder. I wink at her. "Relax, Jen. I'm good." I unhook the blaze-cutter I have strapped to my back and lift it over my head.

Blake grins at me as he takes the heavy tool. "Hey now, that's a plan!" He grips the cutter under one arm, clinging to the ledge with the other as he manoeuvres himself into a reasonable position. I'm glad he's got more muscle than me because I wouldn't be able to one-hand it. "Better get her back." He says, lifting his chin to indicate the girl in the window.

She's watching us, her eyes wide. I gesture for her to get back and she takes several steps backward. Almost soundlessly, the plasma cutter makes light work slicing through the metal remaining against the rim of the glass.

"Look there," Blake says, lifting his chin again to point to some harsh metal scoring against the frame. The corner of his lips lift in a half grin. "This girl's really something. Probably planned on digging her own way out of there. Coming out the way we're going in."

Jenin leans forward, peering at the scratches in the metal. "At least she won't argue about having to climb down with us if she was planning an exit this way anyway."

I smile because they're right and it's pretty cool that we're actually pulling off this rescue. She's just an otherworld chit, friend of Bellamy or not, so it's not like we have any particular loyalty or cause to saving her. Of course, the Faithful do have a loyalty to Bellamy. But since we know he was taken to the city, it's the young girl and her droid I thought we'd be freeing before the Stalkers could kill them.

I glance in the window again. The older girl is fussing with the droid. Her fingers move so fast across the console that I wonder if she can possibly have a sense of what she's typing. Blake makes a final cut in the glass and the frame falls away. I swing back before it cracks me one. Jenin gasps, swinging to the side, and Blake leans back. The glass drops out and we watch as it plummets down the length of the tower and crashes to the ground far below us. It shatters into a scatter of shards. The noise of it is almost nothing compared to the blaring screech coming from the droid.

Instead of waiting for the hot metal to cool, I leverage myself and swing down into the room from above. My feet plant on the floor with a heavy thud and this time I'm almost glad of the racket the bot is making. "Shut it up!" I say, rushing forward.

"I'm trying!" Her fingers are still scrawling across the droid's console. She shakes her head. "Nothing but a bug-riddled scrap rocket."

The droid's face lights up in a scatter of blue symbols that fizzle and fade to nothing but two round orbs. They blink. "What in the nine-voids, it's a Sentient?"

"Oh, thank all of Nar. Hart, can you hear me?"

It tilts its head. "Affirmative." Then, before it can say more, another scatter of blips and bleeps jangle

125

from it. "Oh, excuse me." It lifts a hand to its face as if covering its mouth. "I appear to have a malfunction."

"No kidding. Can you at least get up? We need to get out of here."

The droid seems to ponder that a moment, then twin blue jets fire up beneath it. The spluttering hover-tech is probably twenty narcycles pre-Shadowfall. At least it's functioning.

The girl turns to me. "Tell me we're getting out of here."

I grin at her and tip my head back to the window. "How are you with heights?"

She laughs and my breath catches. I lick my chapping lips, wondering at it, as she says, "I've no idea." The jangle of the door freaks us both out and we glance back at it as it swings open. Hanzor's ugly head seems to precede the rest of him into the room.

"What the baull-scat?" he cries. "Tye! You sly shadow-compy. What the hell?" He turns and shouts down the corridor behind him, "Guards! She's escaping!"

Quick to react, the girl says, "Can't be worse than my last meal." She nudges the platter of food, flicking it with a nimble foot. It flips up and splatters across the front of Hanzor's chest. He swipes the tray away with a splutter as she darts to the window. The metal is still red with heat in places but cooled in others.

"Careful, it's hot."

"Grips are here and here," Blake says as she steps close to the frame.

She nods. Then, with an agile gracefulness, she swings herself out of the window and onto the ledge below. She glances back at the robot, Hart. "Can you follow?" she asks, glancing behind him as Hanzor snarls and reaches for the weapon at his hip.

"Affirmative." The droid jets slightly, then proceeds to hover over the edge of the window frame and horizontally down the surface of the sphere as if it were as easy as hovering across the floor.

"Magnetic?"

"Must be," she says. We both glance back as a rush of guards charge into the room. Hanzor's grip tightens around his plasma pulser as he straightens and levels the weapon at me. No more time to waste. I jump out the window, gripping the ledge with my fingers. A flash of searing plasma flashes past above me.

"Come on!" Jenin and Blake are already moving. Hart leads the way, able to move down the building's struts and spokes as if it's a straight path. He seems completely oblivious to the horde of men after us. I glance back to see Hanzor roaring from the window.

"Get them you daft fools! They're not worth a staple if you let them escape!"

Several guards climb over the ledge above us and begin to move down the building. They move swiftly and I start to worry that we're not moving fast enough. "Come on!" I dart and weave between the ledges. My fingers are still aching from the climb up. My legs are on fire. My breath is heavy, fast, and rasping against the chill air and haze of murk.

Ahead of me, the girl shivers. Each move seems to take more and more out of her and she's slowing. I catch up, passing her slightly. "Next grip is just to your right, footfall about two inches down. That's it, you've got it," I call. She nods, her face full of gratitude as I guide her down the best path.

We both gasp and lean in close against the cold metal as a swoop of wings glides close to our heads. Claws rasp on the metal, then the creature launches again. It grinds the metal beneath its claws as it takes off.

"Eagrims!" I hiss.

The flock squawks and hisses with high-pitched echo-sonics. I freeze and hope that the girl does the same. Risking a glance up I see her frozen in place. She quivers, her eyes wide and scared. Even from here, I can feel her mind racing. In the distance, another eagrim howls. I whisper up to her, "Quiet your mind. Their sonics pick up your movement but lesser beasts also sense your emotions. Still your thoughts."

She draws a long breath and closes her eyes. As she releases the air in her lungs, her quivering arms steady. I grin, admiring her grit and control. She's got this. She's good.

The men above us shout. Clearly, they don't have quiet minds. I sneak a glance, see them wave their arms to ward off the giant winged beasts. A splatter of blood slicks down on us as an eagrim sinks thick fangs into a guard and wrenches his body away from the tower.

Another guard misses a step and plummets past us. His body connects with Hart, slamming into the back of the droid. They both tear away from the tower and freefall to the ground. Metal and meat hit the ground with a sickening crunch. The girl freezes.

I shake my head and say, "We've got to keep moving." She shakes her head. "Look at me," I say, willing her to look down at me. When her strange eyes fix on mine, I'm suddenly not sure what I was going to say. My breathing catches so I force myself to concentrate on each slow breath. I tune out the frenzy of the eagrims feasting above. Instead, I focus on her, on the next step. "One step at a time, follow me, move where I move." She nods and we both trace a path down the tower.

Beneath us, Jenin and Blake touch the ground before we do. They glance back up to the men scrambling down the side of the building. Plasma pulses burst through the sky but we're not the targets. Instead, the eagrims soar and glide to avoid the blasts. They swoop, claiming feast upon feast. Heavy bodies take flight in their talons as they carry the Stalkers off to their distant nests. Some men still move steadily on, climbing down the tower and away from the chaos of their comrades. Some move more cautiously than others.

I feel the ground under my feet and reach out a hand to help the girl touch the surface. She stumbles into my arms as she lands.

"I've got you." I swallow, surprised at how good it feels to have her in my arms. She's slim, her body cool in my arms. My chin brushes the soft silk of her hair. Some hint of madness suggests that I just stand there, holding her, but I steady her on her feet and step away.

Ke-am nudges forward, dropping his head to rub his snout against us. She gasps and moves to step back, but I reach to steady her again. I don't think she's quite got her feet under her.

"It's okay. This is Ke-am. He's our ride." She nods and I help her mount him.

"Wait! Hart."

She moves to dismount again but I shake my head. "No, sit tight. I'll get him."

"Forget him," Jenin calls, "He's just a droid. He'll be forbidden in the City anyway. We've got to go!" She points at the handful of guards still fending off eagrims on the tower above us.

The girl glares at Jenin. "We can't leave him. He's my–" she pauses as if she's not exactly sure what to call him and instead says, "I need him."

Jenin sighs and mounts up on her tiolf as Blake joins me. Together, we strap the droid to one of the tiolf kits, Farlem. The little tiolf seems to feel quite proud about carrying a passenger. He prances in place as I try to tie off the final binding. "Hold still, buddy." He quivers but I get the strap tied.

I turn back to Ke-am. The girl is settled tight against his shoulder blades. She clings to his fur as I climb up behind her. Blake has already joined Jenin, both mounted on Ke-am's mate, Selnar. Their kits stalk around us, gazing up at the guards and eagrims. One munches on the mangled corpse of the Stalker who missed his footing.

"Come on! We've only got a small window before they finish off what's left of those eagrims and come after us," Blake says. I nod, nudging Ke-am, who lopes into long strides away from the tower and back out into the Shadowland. Selnar and the kits match pace beside us. The girl, her energy spent, is heavy in my tired arms. I tighten my grip around her. Ke-am's broad shoulders cradle us as we cover the furlongs between the Outer Rim and the nearest entrance to the City Below.

14

Bringing Home Strays

Niah

I try to keep my eyes open as we charge through the shadows. My heart is racing from the escape. Behind my eyes, I can still see the strange warped faces of the eagrims. Blood sticks in my hair and down my back. It mingles with dust and dirt. I feel like I haven't washed in orbits. Which, I realise, is probably true. I swallow back the spit in my mouth and hug tighter to the soft fur of the tiolf. His pace slows several furlongs from the ring of spheres and I sit up.

Behind me, I can feel the boy's thighs brushing my legs. His knees grip the tiolf beneath us and he guides the beast with confident gestures. "Where are we going?" I ask, but I'm not sure he'll tell me.

"The City Below." I don't really know what that means but I nod anyway. The boy turns to call out to his friends, "Southwest, core three?"

The burly guy calls back, "Yeah, Tye, core three."

"We have a problem," the girl calls.

"What is it, Jenin?"

"A swarm of chortessen."

The boy they'd called Tye turns to Jenin sharply. "Chortessen? Where?"

"They're about three klicks southeast. We should be able to slight past them but we might need to veer westerly."

"Call Farlem back this way," the other boy says. "That kit is far too curious and confident, Jenin. I don't like the way he strays."

The girl nods. "You go on, Tye. We'll round on Farlem and get the kits home."

I feel the dip of his chin as the boy nods. The tiolf beneath us veers off slightly. The other two carry on as we split away.

"Jenin and Blake won't be far behind. They just need to reign in the tiolf kits. They're not as well trained as Ke-am and Selnar so they get a bit rambunctious. I'm Tye by the way." He lifts his hand to me in greeting and I dip my head in response. When I don't give him my name, he says, "Well, you're not Bellamy. Do you have a name?"

I pause, then nod. "Niah." Something in his features feels so familiar. I try to remember where I've seen his honey hair and brown eyes before.

He smiles. "Nice to meet you, Niah." Tye pauses and I think that might be the end of our conversation but then he adds, "You do look a lot like him."

I swallow. "Yeah, so I've been told."

"And you came down in a starship. I saw it." I nod. Although they were statements, I knew they were also questions, but I didn't have any answers for him.

"What about Hart?" I ask instead.

He sighs. "Your robot might cause some problems. There hasn't been much tech allowed. Not since the Shadowfall when the Lord built the cities of light as havens for all of Nar. Now the cities have the only tech allowed although there's plenty of it in them. But no droids. We do our own work."

"We do too, but I guess–" I'm not really sure what I want to say so I shrug.

"He matters to you?"

"He and Wish are all I have." The boy nods and I get a sense that he recognises that loneliness and loyalty.

"Well, now you'll have the Faithful."

"The Faithful?"

"Sure. I mean, you might not be Bellamy but with a starship and his face, maybe you know something of him." I try to keep the wariness out of my face as he talks but he laughs and raises his hands. "No, don't worry. I'm not going to try prying anything out of you. My job is done just getting you away from the Stalkers."

"The Stalkers?"

"Yeah, they're the boundary guards. They mark the shadows between the City of Light and the Outer Rim. Although sometimes they harvest this side of the rim like they did with you. You fell foul of a pit trap. Normally, they catch stray chortessen because they fetch serious staples for food and fabric. I imagine it about blew Hanzor's eyes out to see you and the other girl. Was that Wish?"

I nod, and swallow the lump in my throat. "They took her."

His chin moves against my hair as he nods. "They'll have taken her to the City of Light. I'm thinking they mistook her for you."

"You mean they mistook her for Bellamy."

"Yeah, that too. And so long as they don't realise their mistake, she'll be okay."

"What about when they do?"

The long pause seems to shout. Then he says, quietly, "Yeah, well, I guess we'll just have to find her before then."

I smile, glancing back at him. "Thanks."

He lifts a shoulder in a depreciative shrug and turns his attention to guiding the tiolf through the darkness. It's an almost effortless task because the beast seems to know the way. Even so, I feel better because it feels like he's on my side. They both are. And with a lesser beast and this strange boy, maybe anything is possible. Maybe we'll find Wish. And maybe we'll manage to complete the mission and save Nar too.

The dark world around us seems like an endless roll of hills and dunes. Before another few furlongs pass, Blake and Jenin catch up to us with the trail of kits in a more or less orderly straggle. I breathe a sigh of relief when I catch sight of Hart still strapped to a young tiolf's back. Tye smiles against my hair and heat rises in my cheeks. "He's fine," he says, "and we're almost there."

I peer forward, wondering if I can see the 'there' he's talking about. Ahead of us, are more hills and dunes. The tiolf beneath us slows his pace. He circles a small flat valley in the dunes around us.

Tye draws him up and slides down his side. The chill of night air down my back makes me shiver. I flush again, realising Tye's body had been keeping me warm.

I glance around at the barren nothingness surrounding us. "Here?"

Tye glances up at me with a grin. "Yep, here. You right to get down?"

My muscles ache and I'm not sure how much strength I have left in me but I grit my teeth and force myself to nod. Gripping the tiolf's fur, I lift my leg over his back and slide down to the ground. The dirt beneath my feet shifts slightly and I brace myself so I won't fall. The cool breeze over the thin weave of my sleeper suit makes me shiver again.

"Here," Tye says, dropping his own black coat over my shoulders. I delve my arms into its warmth and pull the cowl over my head. It smells like him. The heat of it – the heat of him – wards off the cold. I glance a shy smile up at him, hoping he can't sense my thoughts, before his attention is drawn away.

Blake jogs toward us and together, he and Tye reach down into the dirt and pull back a hefty shingle of wood. I feel my mouth drop open as I realise they're uncovering a secret entrance to what must be a very big chamber under the ground. There's no light from the darkness below. What little light penetrates the Shadowlands shows only a glimpse of stairs leading into the blackness beyond.

Jenin whistles to the tiolf and they lumber

toward us. "Steady," she calls to them as they loll into her like overeager chortessa pups.

Blake gives an odd pitched hoot into the hollow. It echoes down what sounds like a very long tunnel. Moments later, an answering squawk sounds back to us. Deccas after, a flicker of torchlight creates a warm glow against the black rock.

"About time, Tye. The ruckus you guys set off at the Outer Rim beat you back here. Lyris has been beside herself." An older man appears through the darkness. His face reflects the light. His dark hair is the same colour as the rocky staircase. His blue eyes remind me of Wish, although his are perhaps a shade or two darker than her icicles.

"Sorry, Tannan," Tye replies, "Wasn't all us, though."

"So I heard. Eagrims. What a night for them to be out hunting, huh?" The older man winks. I sense there's more to what he's saying but I'm not sure what it is.

Tye raises an eyebrow. "From the northeast ridge?" Tannan nods. "Nicely done! Although you played it fast and loose with our lives, Tannan. How could you be sure they wouldn't attack us?"

Tannan shakes his head. "You? You've been a shadow-compy since those eagrims were fledglings. You and Janin between you could handle a few eagrims and probably have them eating out of your hands. You've got the quietest mind I've ever heard."

Tye gives his cute half smile to that but I glance at Tannan, wondering if I heard him correctly. He turns his blue-eyed gaze on me as if sensing my thoughts.

"What's this then?"

I bite my lip, not sure if he's asking me. Tye steps closer to me. His fingers brush my back, as if he had planned to touch me there and changed his mind. "This is Niah. She's the one I told you about."

Tannan turns his gaze on Tye with a frown. "You said you'd seen the spitting image of Bellamy. Not a girl who could pass for his daughter."

Tye lifts a shoulder. "With a furlong between you, light from behind, and the Captain's coat over her shoulders you wouldn't pick it yourself." Tannan returns his eyes to me and I lift my chin at the way he scrutinises my face.

"I'm not Bellamy," I say, as if I need to clarify that point.

Tannan tilts his head. "No, I suppose not, but you're darn close. And from a starship, Tye tells me. The Elixr? Not many ships would carry a name like that."

I glance away. "No, I suppose not."

A sudden splutter and whoop startles us all and we turn to see the young tiolf lope toward us. On his back, head spinning and face screen a swirl of confused symbols and letters, is a very worked up and noisy Hart.

"What's this then?" Tannan asks. "Tech?"

Tye lifts his hands to his ears. "Noisy tech. The derpy bot makes a nine-voids worth of racket. No idea how we're going to hide him from the Stalkers. Might set off an alert through the whole of the Outer Rim if he ever got close to the city."

Hart's face clears and his eye orbs blink into place. His hover jets flare and the tiolf startles, whimpers, and tries to dart away, but with Hart still strapped to his back everywhere he dashes the robot goes with him. "I do believe I'm experiencing some minor turbulence issues," Hart says. I sigh because clearly he's still not in his right mind, or circuits.

Jenin steps forward and calls to the tiolf. "Farlem, here boy." The tiolf stalks toward her, his tail down and ears flat. As he reaches her side he tips his head to give Hart a low growl. "Hey, none of that boy. He's our friend." She tugs on the straps binding Hart in place and the droid sinks from the tiolf's back and clunks to the ground.

"Oh dear," he says, righting himself with a push of his hands and a flare of his jets. Once upright he blinks his eye orbs and glances around. "Ah, Narians. Hail and well met. I am Harttade, a Hybrid Autonomous Research, Telemetry, Teleportation, and Defence Engine."

Tannan raises an eyebrow and turns his gaze back on me. "A Sentient? Those were outlawed near to two hundred narcycles ago." I swallow and bite my lip.

"Outlawed?" Hart blusters. "Outlawed! But I am state-of-the-art! A necessary component of the function of the Elixr and our quest for the cure." He stutters into silence with a blink. His head turns first one way and then the other as he takes in the five Narians in the room. "Please disregard my statements. They are classified." He turns to me. "Niah, we must return to the ship."

I shake my head. "We have to get Wish back."

Hart blinks in that dull-faced way he has about him. Then, with a hiss of a sigh, he says, "She is not necessary to our mission. You are still capable of completing the objective."

I shake my head. "We needed help, remember? Maybe these people can help us."

He falls silent and even the twin orbs of his eyes disappear. I start to wonder if he is malfunctioning until he finally blinks his eyes open again. "Affirmative. Proceed with mission."

"Okay then," Tannan says, shaking off what he's heard.

Tye steps forward, putting a hand on Tannan's arm. "The other one, they mistook her for Bellamy because of the coat. We should go get her, too."

Tannan grimaces. "More strays, Tye?"

Jenin frowns. "Didn't you hear the droid, Tannan? They're on Bellamy's mission. They came in the Elixr. They have the cure. This is what the Shadows and the Faithful have hoped and prayed for these past two hundred narcycles."

His lips stiff, Tannan nods. "Fine. Lyris would kill me if I didn't at least tell her about this. You know, Tye, the things we Faithful do for you. Sometimes I think you ask too much."

Tye places a hand on Tannan's arm. He meets the man's gaze, sharing an unspoken word before saying, "You know I don't ask for more than I give."

Tannan nods. "Yeah," he says quietly. "And for all you give, you're worth the Lord's ransom." One corner of his lips lift in a wry smile. "Which I guess is exactly what you're worth now." He winks. "So, what do you need?"

Blake, who has been quiet up to now, runs a hand through his murk-stained hair. "Right now, the most important thing is probably to get us all cleaned up, fed, and rested." He turns to Tye and waves his hand up and down to indicate the state of us. "You won't get past the Outer Rim covered in eagrim's slop, and if you're set on rescuing the other one then you'll want to head into the City of Light."

"Right," says Tye. I bite my lip, not wanting to wait but not really having much choice.

15

The Lord of Light

Niah

The City Below stretches on under the ground. The haze of the torch casts strange dancing shadows against the black rock of the walls. We weave through the dark pits for what feels like several narcycles, but is probably only a few deccas. Eventually, it broadens out into chambers and rooms. Torches flicker, casting a dim light on the faces of the few people we pass.

At first I gaze around me, wondering at the strange city that seems to have been carved into the hard black rock beneath the Shadowland. But whispers and gasps start to echo through the chambers, and even the name seems to precede us down the halls, stirring the Narians from their beds. I sink further and further into the shadow of Tye's coat.

"Bellamy!"

"Is it really him?"

"It's Bellamy."

"Come to save us."

The nameless faces of a reverent people seem to swell around us. I shake my head. "I'm not him, really." But Tannan keeps us moving too quickly to give me a chance to refute their claims.

Tye steps close to me, lifting an arm as if warding off the reaching hands of the Faithful. "There's no point denying it, Niah. They've spent generations living on the hope of Bellamy's return. You wear his face. To them, you are our saviour."

I shake my head. "I'm not him."

"No, but you're the closest we'll find, aren't you?"

Tears blur my vision and grow angry at my own weakness. If I really were Bellamy, I wouldn't be a simpering mess of emotion and exhaustion. The waves of hopeful but desperate energy rising up in the people around is like a crushing weight. When they start dropping to their knees, touching their heads to the floor, and chanting in a rhythmic cadence I feel the tension rising in the air.

"How curious," Hart says in his bland, understated way.

My head throbs as if keeping time with the chant. It's like a drum, thrumming through me with every pitch and warble in the air. My muscles ache from the cold of the prison cell, the chaos of the climb, the long hard ride, and now this endless walk. Every nerve in my body is spent. I pitch slightly, tripping over my own feet. Tye reaches out, catching me in his arms.

"Hey, you okay?" he asks. His voice is warm and soft. It's soothing against the harshness ash and smoke haze surrounding us.

My mind grows more and more fuzzy. I shake my head, trying to clear it. "I don't think…" And I guess I don't, because my tongue stops cooperating and my eyes refuse to open.

I feel Tye lift me up in his arms. He carries me forward but I don't know how far we travel because against his shoulder, with the soft beat of his heart in my ear, the world falls away again. Deep in my gut, I curse this sickness and long for my sister.

Wish

Moonlight swirls in the sky. It casts a wash of pale light through a growing canopy of clouds. The City of Light is a wonder of arched white buildings soaring up to the artificial sky. The carriage moves slowly along the street, creaking with age or weight or both. Eventually, it pulls up in front of a towering building of glass, crystal, and shimmering white fibreglass plating. I can barely pick up my mouth up from the floor of the carriage as I gaze out of the window. Beside me, the guard chuckles.

"Right you are to be awed like that. The Palace downright awes us all, I reckon. But come on, don't want to be keeping the Lord waiting." He reaches past me to push open the door and then grips my arm as he leads us out. I want to pull away, but the swarm of people around us makes me wary. Where can I possibly go and how will I ever find Niah in all of this? I decide to play along, bide my time until a better escape option comes along, or Niah and Hart find me first.

I lift my chin as he hauls me up the stairs of the Palace. I march beside him, trying to match my footsteps to his larger ones without tripping over the stairs. He nods to the guards at the front entrance but moves on without stopping. Then he barks a command in the reception hall. "Let the Lord know I've brought Bellamy to him."

"Please wait in the parlour," the steward responds. He waves a negligent hand at a door along the far wall.

"Right." The guard stalks us both through the door and we enter a beautifully furnished waiting room. I hold my shoulders back as he pushes me forward. I just manage to keep my feet under me. I spin, ready to lay into him, then remember that I'm supposed to be Bellamy. I wipe the anger away and replace it with a cool air of detachment.

As the wait extends to what must be nearly a factor, I find myself pacing in front of the windows that look out on the glory of the city. Eventually, the steward comes into the room. I glance at him, wondering where Lord Oliver might be, and if he'll ever join us.

"The Lord is in Virreal and asks that you join him."

I furrow my brow. "Virreal?"

The guard sighs. "You have some rigs set up for us then?"

"Of course, Thomis. If you'll both follow me."

He leads us up the main staircase and down a long stretch through a wing of the Palace. The building is a strange mix of classic marble stonework, high tech glass, fibreglass, and even electronics. The lighting is built directly into the panels of the wall. In parts, the Palace reminds me of the Elixr, with her fine lines and the harmonious blend of function and feature.

As we enter yet another room, the extraordinary display of technology reminds me of the sleeper pods, or the plush chairs of the morning break room, or even the several workstations in the lab on board the starship.

Several comfortable chairs are twinned together and span the length of the room. Each pair is hooked up to its own processor with an array of cables.

Thomis makes his way directly to the nearest chair. He settles himself back into it and reaches over for a headset, then begins to plug himself in, which is odd to me because even in the sleeper pod nothing had been specifically attached to my body the way this headset seems to attach to him. He winces as it clips into place over his ears, eyes, nose, and mouth. He tugs on a pair of gloves and then turns his head in a full range of motion before settling back against the chair.

The steward beside me sighs, and gestures to the chair next to him. "This way, please. The Lord is waiting."

"But–" I glance at the chair, uncertain. Seeming to sense what my hesitation is about, the steward moves to the various parts and begins setting them up for me. I climb into the chair and settle my back against it. The steward straps me into the strange device.

I gasp as a whole new world seems to take shape

behind my eyes. In place of the white walls and pristine, almost sterile quality of the City of Light, appears a vast, multi-hued forest of beautiful flowers, trees, and life. I find myself standing beside Thomis as he gazes around and then shrugs.

"Well, I've been to better places," he mumbles. "Come on, it must be this way."

He leads us down a path through the trees and we break out into the sunlight beside a cascading waterfall and a cool lake. Walking along the water's edge, is a young man. His hair is only a hint or two darker than my own and as he turns to look at us, I feel like I'm looking in a mirror. My own eyes gaze back at me. The same jet of ice-blue, even the same curve of nose. The traces of Lord Oliver's well-kept facial hair also can't hide the familiar weight of his lower lip. I glance down, hiding my own face.

"Ah! My brother, Captain Jacob Bellamy," Lord Oliver drawls. "You've finally returned."

Brother? I blink, glancing up in confusion. Lord Oliver's gaze narrows. He crosses the distance between us to look more carefully at my face.

"Not Jacob?" He turns on Thomis, his lips tight and eyes piercing. "This is not Captain Bellamy, you fool!"

Beside me, Thomis splutters. Lord Oliver lifts a hand and Thomis begins choking on nothingness. "Lord–" he hacks between gasps of shallow air. "I can explain." The Lord thrusts his hand and Thomis is flung backward as if thrown several feet by a very strong force.

He pushes himself up, clawing at the floor, and sucks in ragged but deep breaths.

147

"Explain then, but your explanation better suffice. Chortessa is hungry."

Thomis groans. He lifts a hand. "My Lord, please, forgive me. She's wearing his coat, and the eyes, they said she had his eyes, his hair, his face. They said it was Bellamy."

"His eyes? His hair? His face? This child! This girl child looks like Captain Bellamy? She looks more like me than she does my brother you pathetic waste of void-scum Narian."

"Lord, I didn't– I just– Hanzor."

"Hanzor? That incompetent oaf. You're in league with Hanzor?"

"No– well yes, he's my– well, no." Thomis' confused jumble seems to make the Lord even more short tempered. "When Hanzor hauled them out of the pit, the other one was wearing the coat. The other Bellamy."

Lord Oliver's gaze narrows at the fumble of Thomis' explanation. "The other one?"

"They must have changed clothes. Switched places. The other one, Bellamy, he must still be in the Cage."

The Lord scowls. "I've already heard about the escape."

Thomis' eyes seem to bulge then and his Adam's apple bobs. "Escape?" he whispers. My heart races with hope. If Niah's escaped, maybe she's coming for me.

Lord Oliver continues, "If you've anything to do with any of that, you'll deserve a fate worse than the one you'll have in the teeth of my beautiful Chortessa." His smile is dark. It sends a shiver of unease down my spine. I feel my stomach flip, unsure of the wisdom of having put myself here in this place. Maybe it would have been smarter to run when I'd had a small, fleeting moment of opportunity on the steps of the Palace.

"Please, please no, my Lord. I had nothing to do with that. Nothing. I serve only you, my Lord. I've always been loyal. I am your man, my Lord. Your man."

"Enough!" Lord Oliver roars. I flinch back as the echo of his voice dances off the trees and waterfall as if echoing from the solid walls of a room. The world around us flickers and blinks. Suddenly, we all stand in the darkness of an earthen pit. The dirt feels gritty beneath my bare feet. I feel a shiver as I sense a greater darkness nearby and spin as the shadows move around us.

"NO! Lord, please! No, no, no." Thomis pleads and whimpers. He is on his hands and knees now. It looks like he is trying to scramble away but is held in place by an invisible hand.

A heavy, rasping breath sounds beside me. I step sideways, startled, but the odd creature doesn't seem to notice me. Its hungry gaze is fixed on Thomis, whose terror is marked all over his face. It's in the acrid stench of his own urine-soaked clothing and the fresh sheen of sweat drenching the collar of his shirt and the pits of his sleeves.

The Lord watches as the beast stalks its prey. His grin is almost affectionate and his chin is lifted in pride as he stands on the sidelines of the beast's lair. "Yes, my beautiful. Enjoy your dinner."

I swallow and bite my lip as I watch. I can't tear

my gaze away, even knowing what is about to happen. Then, as suddenly as the room had come up around us, the invisible force holding Thomis in place disappears and he moves. Scrambling through the dirt.

He pushes himself to his feet and runs a short way before slamming into an invisible wall. He turns, fleeing in another direction. He turns in circles, always away from the beast as he tries to escape. In every direction he faces barrier after barrier.

Meanwhile, the creature stalks him. It snuffles through its nose. It turns on strong, lanky legs. Turns its head and ears as if listening to every movement Thomis makes.

Finally, as if tired of toying with its food, it lunges forward. It grips Thomis in its teeth, paws raised up to score down Thomis' chest with thick, sharp claws. Ribbons of blood spurt to the surface. The chortessa grips Thomis with a clenched jaw and shakes him. The man shudders in the beast's grip. He cries out, over and over again, until the teeth of the beast close around his neck. It chokes the air out of him before breaking the surface of the skin and ripping out the man's throat.

I turn away, but can't stop seeing the carnage of torn flesh, spurting blood, and raw bone. I can't block out the acrid smell of sweat and gore mixing with earth. It's so crude and vivid that I taste it on my tongue. I also can't block out the sound of the Lord's almost lustful panting and the soft chuckle in his rich voice. My stomach swirls and I feel like I should throw up but I can't. It's almost as if, in this world, my physical body is detached from my mind.

As Thomis stops thrashing and the chortessa settles in to devour his carcass, Lord Oliver sighs beside me. "Well," he says, "that was a mild entertainment." He turns to me. "And you? Should I feed you to my Chortessa, as well?"

I fix him with my best Bellamy stare. His eyes narrow so I suspect it was convincing. He presses a button on a band on his wrist and moments later the world around us swirls again. Twin doors open into the pit and four Stalkers trail into the room. They glance warily at the chortessa. It continues to chew and crunch on the remains of Thomis. The youngest of the men shudders then forces his gaze to the Lord.

"My Lord?" asks the most senior of the guards.

"I want the so-called 'Chosen One' brought to me within the next twenty-four factors. Bring me Captain Jacob Bellamy or bring me his head, and be sure to let those rebel traitor Shadow-scum know that this girl will be Chortessa's next meal if my brother is not brought before me by this time tomorrow." The guard taps his shoes together and salutes, then the four turn and march out of the room. The doors swing closed behind them.

Lord Oliver turns to me. His face is lit with a dark half-smile. "Let's see if my brother cares for you enough to come before me."

16

Haven of the Faithful

Tye

The gasps of concern around us have me worried. With so many people already passing rumours of Bellamy's return, the last thing we need in the energy of the City Below is for word to get around that something is wrong with the saviour. While the Faithful are mostly a kind people, their fanaticism makes them unpredictable.

"Is she okay?" Tannan asks. His gaze is worried. He quickly shepherds us into a dorm room away from prying eyes. I march forward, carrying her down the hall and across the room. Tannan gives a short order to Blake, who nods and closes the door behind us, giving us a degree of privacy.

Niah feels like a wisp in my arms. She is so slight and dainty. I can carry even her fully unconscious body without losing breath. I press my lips together, unable to answer Tannan's question. Instead, I sit down on the bunk and keep her cradled in my lap, her head on my shoulder. I stroke back fine pale strands of hair from her face and gaze down on her. Her dark eyelashes brush the soft flush of her skin.

Tannan moves forward and, doctor-like, takes a quick stock of her vitals. Her breath is shallow but even, her pulse bounding but regular.

Her features are so fragile that I wonder how I could have ever mistaken her for Captain Bellamy. Her face is flushed but restful. My heart aches, fearing a death upon her but the soft pink in her lips reassures me. So does the heat coming from her although that in itself is worrying.

The door opens and Jenin darts into the room. I hear the stir of voices outside that show our dramatic entrance hasn't gone unnoticed. Blake's strong voice takes command. "Stand back, please." He pulls the door closed and the sounds fall to a vibrating murmur.

"Here." Jenin passes me a damp wash cloth and sets a bowl of cool water on the bedside table. "Karel will bring some food, something light but hardy. These will help bring down her temperature. I don't know what else we can do for her here."

Tannan nods. "We won't know until we can find out more."

Jenin shakes her head. "I don't want to draw bloods or make assertions without at least having the chance to talk to her, so we'll give her some time."

Tannan nods. "Okay then, but if she doesn't wake by morning, I want you to take her to the infirmary."

I stroke the damp cloth across her brow. "Is that really necessary?" I wonder what could have happened to her. Surely she's not so fragile that our climb could have wiped her out so completely. "You don't think it's just exhaustion?"

Jenin pauses, gazing down on Niah, then shakes her head. "I'd almost agree but it doesn't justify her temperature. I'm worried she's experiencing encephalitis but so far, her pupils are responsive. I don't believe she's in any immediate danger. Did she say anything?"

I shake my head. What little she did say reveals nothing useful so it's not worth repeating. I dampen the cloth in the cool water again, then wipe her face with even strokes across her forehead and down the sides of her temples. Her eyelids flutter. I catch my breath but she still doesn't wake.

A few deccas pass before Jenin sighs. "I'll leave you. I need to get the kits settled in. Call me if there's anything I can do to help."

I look up to her. "What did you do with her droid?"

"Blake sent it to Lyris. It'll be upstairs in the lab by now."

Tannan nods. "Good. I'll check in with you in a few factors, Tye. Hopefully rest will do her some good."

Jenin pauses at the door. "Keep trying to bring her temperature down, Tye. That will help."

I nod but she and Tannan don't wait for my response before they both leave the room. I hear the edges of Jenin muttering something to Blake as she pulls the door closed with a quiet click, then everything else is muffled.

I gaze down on Niah and feel an aching worry in the pit of my gut. For some reason, I care about this beautiful otherworld girl. Even with her eyes closed, I remember their strange glow and the hint of a sad knowing within them. I remember the soft melody of her laugh.

I stroke the damp cloth over her skin. Her cheeks, her neck, her collar. Over time, she cools and the colour in her face softens to a gentle pink. Her breath, shallow for so many heartbeats, seems to gain strength.

Eventually, she stirs in my arms. Her eyelids flutter open. She gazes up at me with confused eyes. I smile, trying to be reassuring. "Hey there, sleepy."

She bites her lip, turning her head as if trying to understand where she is. "Where–" She stops, and moves to sit up. I help ease her upright because I can't exactly justify just keeping her on my lap. I don't want her to move too far so, as she settles on the bed beside me, I let my leg rest close to hers.

"We're in the City Below. It's a haven for the Faithful, the Shadows, or both."

She blinks and I can tell she doesn't really understand what I'm telling her. I try to imagine how new this must all seem for an otherworlder.

"You're somewhere safe, Niah. We can help you."

"Help me?"

I nod. "With your mission, your quest? Or with..." I let my words fall because I'm not sure how to ask her if she's sick. I imagine the question is all over my face.

She bites her lip again, which is adorable. A white spot appears and I want to smooth it away with the pad of my thumb but that would be weird. We've only just met. Still, I can't help feeling like I know her on some level. She feels familiar, as if our hearts have known each other longer than our own lifetimes.

She gazes at me so long that I feel like maybe I should break the silence, then she does. "Your eyes are brown."

I flush, but nod.

"I've never seen brown eyes before."

I chuckle because it's something so inane and random, but somehow it seems like her to notice. It breaks the tension. I reach out to brush a stray strand of hair from her face. "I've never seen eyes like yours, either. At least, not in person, just in pictures."

"Of Bellamy?"

I nod.

"I'm not him."

"I know." She sighs and I feel braver now. "Are you sick, Niah?"

She drops her chin and looks down at her fingers, grasping them together. I feel my breath freeze in that moment of hesitation because I suddenly realise that I don't really want to know the truth. I want to believe she's perfect, and perfectly healthy.

She lifts a shoulder and raises her eyes to mine again. "I don't know. Well, I don't understand it. Hart says there's something wrong with me, a mistake in my genes." She pauses, glancing away.

"I get really, really sick sometimes."

"And you pass out?"

She nods. "Sometimes."

I lean forward, catching her chin. As I gaze into her face I feel an ache in my heart. "It's bad, isn't it?" She nods and I hate myself for the pain I feel inside. How can I care so much about someone I barely know?

She reaches forward and strokes a tear from my cheek. In her gentle gaze, I see the echo of my yearning. It's as if she's as conscious as I am about the fragility of it all. The fleetingness of this moment, this heartbeat. I reach up and catch her hand against my cheek. She's sitting so close to me that I can feel her breath on my lips.

"We'll save you," I whisper. The shimmer of tears on her lashes tugs on my heart. I pull her close against my chest. "Hey, don't cry. We'll find a way, Niah. I can save you."

She shakes her head but doesn't pull away. Instead, she leans into me and I hold her close. I feel the dampness of her tears through my shirt and drop my head to hers as she sobs. Eventually, she pulls back slightly. She lifts her face to mine.

My breath catches. Her pale pink lips are so perfect and sweet. With a soft groan, I lean forward. We barely brush, but my heart staggers. She doesn't pull away, so I taste her more deeply and we cling to each other. I pull back and she gazes up at me, her pale eyes wide. I wonder what she's thinking, what she's feeling.

She swallows, closing her eyes. She shakes her head as if there are no words that can express what dances between us. Then she leans forward, tucking herself beneath my chin. Her small body fits in the curve of mine. I hold her close against me. She's so fragile and delicate that I'm almost afraid to breathe with her in my arms, but I can't bring myself to let her go so I lean back against the wall and just hold her close.

17

Avatars And Identities

Niah

My heart races with a reckless joy that dances strangely within me. I barely know this boy and yet something about him feels so familiar. I can't help trusting him completely. Just like the instant connection I'd felt to Wish, my sister, this boy creates an echo within me as if I've known him all my existence. It's insane but undeniable.

Held in the curve of his arms, leaning into the warmth of his chest, his heart beats beneath my ear. I feel like I'm where I belong. For the first time, I'm not afraid of my own existence. Right now, in this decca, I feel I'm exactly where I was always meant to be.

His fingers stroke my hair. I'm still so tired. I wonder how long I've been asleep, or passed out, really, I guess. Wondering makes me worry and I graze my teeth across my bottom lip. Tye brushes his fingers down my arm. I breathe him in. He smells earthy and real, as if his very being were tied to the planet in the same way mine is tethered to the stars.

I feel myself dozing on and off against his shoulder. Time passes but I don't know how long he sits here with me, just holding me. I wish I had the strength to pull away, to talk to him, but even the silence feels right and my body keeps dragging me back to sleep so I give in to these stolen moments. The world around us will demand more of me soon enough. Wish still hovers on the outskirts of my thoughts but, just at this moment, the best I can do is rest.

Eventually, the door creaks open. Tye and I both sit up, putting distance between us. Tannan's blue eyes seem particularly perceptive as he comes into the room. Tannan is trailed by an older and more world-wearied man carrying a tray heaped with steaming food. Large bowls of dark purple soup with thick loaves of bread. The smell is divine, like nothing I've ever smelled before and yet again, so familiar.

"Ah, she's awake," Tannan says. His words are kind, almost caring, but professional. "Tye tells me your name is Niah?" I nod. "I should have introduced myself properly earlier. I'm Tannan and I'm in charge of keeping Shadows like Tye out of the eye and arm of the Stalkers. This is Karel, he's in charge of keeping the Faithful fed in the City Below."

Tye grins and reaches out for one of the bowls Karel has to offer. "He does a fine job of it too." Tye digs into the food with relish and I wonder when he's last seen a decent feed. My own stomach growls, reminding me that I've skipped a meal or two myself. I breathe in the aromas of the still steaming food.

Karel smiles at me but rather than handing me a bowl, he arranges the side table, moving the bowl of water over to the dresser and pulling the table closer to me so that he can lay the food out on top of it. He hands me a spoon. "Earth bulb stew with sapper root scalloped in fresh mamot milk. I considered adding compy meat but wasn't sure if you would take to it; not everyone does."

Nothing of what he says makes much sense to me. I have no idea what earth bulbs, sapper roots, or compy meat are, but since the stew smells delicious, I nod my head and tug apart the loaf of bread to dip chunks of it into the thick liquid. The taste of it on my tongue tingles with hints of familiarity and I realise how very hungry I am.

Tannan watches Tye and me devour our food for a few moments and then pulls up a chair opposite us. "I've got some news." Tye lifts his head, pausing between chews. Tannan raises a hand. "Actually, it's more good than bad. We know where they've taken the girl."

I look up from my meal and swallow my mouthful before saying, "Her name is Wish. She's my sister."

Tannan gives a thoughtful nod, then continues. "Well, she's currently a 'guest' of the Lord. They have her at the Palace."

"The Palace?" Tye says, "I don't know how you think that's good news."

"Well, at least we aren't left wondering."

"And when you say guest, I assume she does not have comfortable lodgings."

"To be honest, I don't know. Word trickles to us through the Stalkers. They are on high alert. Rumour is that one of their own became a meal for the Lord's beast and he's asked them to make it known in certain circles that the girl is next if Bellamy isn't delivered to him by factor twenty-two tomorrow."

My heart sinks. "But Bellamy doesn't exist." Tye and Tannan's eyes both settle on me. I can see their minds ticking away. Their scrutiny makes my skin crawl. "I'm not him!"

"Of course you're not," Tannan agrees, "but you could pass for it if they don't look too close."

Tye shakes his head. "The Lord will look close, Tannan. And we can't hand her over to him. Besides, he'd likely as not arrange for all of us to hang if we tried to deliver her to him."

"Or become a lesser beast chew toy," Karel adds.

Tye continues as if Karel hadn't spoken. "You know he wouldn't take kindly to the return of the Elixr."

I furrow my brow and turn to him. "Why not? I thought everyone was waiting for the cure?"

Tye sighs. "A lot has happened in two hundred narcycles. Lord Oliver has become very comfortable in his place as ruler."

Tannan nods. "The Lord has found a power and freedom in what he has created here. Accepting that Nar might be cured of the shadows means giving all Narians a chance to choose a life outside of the City of Light. Without the people, his city falls."

"What do you mean?"

Tye leans past me as he places his now empty bowl on the table. "The City of Light exists in a very careful balance of power. For the Inner Circle, those with enough staples to guarantee a lifetime of access to Virreal, there is a certainty in knowing they have an assured place in the adventure kingdom. They get to live out their dreams and create the peoples of the Lord's other worlds."

I feel like I'm getting more and more confused with every word but I try to make sense of it all in my head.

Tye continues, "Most of the city is Outer Circle. They make up the workforce that keeps the city running. If you aren't in either the Inner or Outer Circle you're outcast. Some will wander into the Shadowlands, becoming Shadow people like me. Others find their way down here to the Faithful."

"Yes," Tannan says, "and with careful negotiation and the trade of staples, there is a degree of crossover between those three levels, but no manner of staples will get a Shadow into the Inner Circle. A Stalker maybe, but not us, not the outcast."

I lick my lips at the last taste of my now finished meal as I push the bowl aside. Karel smiles down on me as he reaches to gather up the dishes.

"So how does this help us rescue Wish?"

Tannan's brow furrows. "Well, it makes things difficult. You see, potentially we could present you as Bellamy. That would get us access to the Inner Circle and the Palace beyond. It would give us a way to get in. Without that, access is almost impossible."

Tye shakes his head. "But it's suicide for all of us. It's not really an option. No sane person delivers themselves to Lord Oliver."

"Right," Tannan says, "and that makes it harder. We can't just walk in. We need Inner Circle credentials. We might even need avatars."

"Avatars?" I ask.

Tannan nods but Tye is the one to explain. "Virreal is a virtual reality. The Lord spends most of his time there and odds are they've taken Wish there as well. We can't get her out unless she chooses to disconnect for herself. If they haven't told her how then she might not be able to. If they've linked her into Virreal, then someone will need to go in after her."

"And avoid the hazards within," Tannan says.

"So," says Tye, "credentials? How do you think we could swing those?"

"Actually, I have an idea about that, but it'll have to wait until morning." He turns to me. "You both need sleep, and Lyris and I will need a few factors to line up some valid codes."

I lean forward. "But what about Wish, and the deadline?"

Tannan puts a hand on my shoulder. "We have time. He won't hurt her while he believes she holds value. Look at you both, dead on your feet. You're no good to her if you can't stay conscious while you rescue her."

I frown, feeling frustrated at being trapped in this failing body. I know that he's right. I sigh.

"Yeah, okay. But first thing in the morning, okay?" Tannan nods. As he and Karel head out the door, Tye moves to stand too. I grip his arm, suddenly afraid to be left alone. "Will you stay?" I know he must see a pathetic desperation in my eyes and I feel stupid being so afraid. I lean forward and whisper, "I'm afraid to close my eyes."

Tye's gaze softens. He gives me a gentle smile and leans back against the wall. "I can stay, if you want me to." Tannan glances back at us and gives Tye a look before closing the door. Tye turns to me. "I'm right here Niah, it's safe to sleep here."

"And you'll wake me up, right? In the morning? I don't want to sleep forever."

"I'll wake you up. I promise."

I lean into him and his arms come around me. He strokes my hair and I know he can feel the tension in my body as I try to let myself fall asleep. The soft, rhythmic beat of his heart against my ear is soothing. I close my eyes, feeling the race of my own heart and will it to match his calmer tempo. I lie, letting the quiet stillness of the night come over me. The gentle brush of Tye's fingers through my hair and down my back, soothes me to sleep.

18

Gone To Pieces

Niah

The halls and stairwell leading up to the lab seem almost deserted now. I wonder what time it must be on the surface. The City Below is a strange mix of dark rock and shimmering metals. It's as if time forgot this place. There is an odd blend of fibreglass and metal, like on the Elixr, mixed with ancient catacombs of the stone and medieval ages. Smoking torches are staggered at intervals along the walls in more established areas.

We wind through several corridors and then up two flights of stairs before reaching what the others called the lab. After the eclectic clutter of the City Below, I'm startled by the modern tech inside.

"Lyris," Tannan says, greeting the tall dark-haired woman that stands with her back to us. "How you doing, Boss?"

She turns, her face wreathed in a smile. It's clear she's in her element here, surrounded by a scatter of tech and completely at home amongst it.

As she steps toward us, I gasp. Hart sits in a jumble of pieces behind her. His face screen is dormant and black. His head is precariously propped so that the wires connecting it to his torso are supported without the column rods that construct his neck. His torso is deconstructed and his interior is spread across the table. His hover thrusters are in parts.

"What have you done!" I cry, rushing forward. I pick up several of the pieces in turn and bite my lip. A clench of tension hits my gut and the breath bursts from my lungs.

"Is it yours?" Lyris asks. "It's magnificent, truly. I haven't seen tech in such good condition outside of the Inner Circle. I mean, it's not perfect, of course. It does show significant signs of age, but since the ban two hundred narcycles ago, the only technology that hasn't fallen to rust and murk is the tech that keeps the City of Light functioning. That's all owned by the Lord so I can never get my hands on it. But this, it's a masterwork of construction. It must have been state-of-the-art in its circuit."

Her rambling voice does little to sooth my nerves. "You've got to put him back together. What were you thinking? We need him!"

Tannan looks down at the jumble of parts. "Chortessa's guts, Lyris. Can you get the darn thing working again?"

"Oh, I, well, I've been fixing him. There's a degree of damage, partly from the fall but, well he's quite aged too, so some of his internals need replacing. I sent Blake and Jenin out to get what I need but it might take several factors at the least before I can have him fully functional."

"But he was working before! He was talking. Can't you at least wake him up?"

"Well, sort of."

Tannan raises an eyebrow. "Sort of? I was counting on the droid tech being able to hack us into the city."

"Well, his primary processor is offline but he has a partial memory backup on this interface, so there are aspects of his program that will run independently from the main unit." Lyris picks up a panel of plating with a screen that reminds me of the tablets Wish and I used on Elixr.

Tye comes forward. He looks down at the tablet, lifting it from Lyris's hands. "This thing is the robot?"

She blinks. "Yes, I suppose so, at least in part. It plays the role of an interface in the short term and contains the base of his coding." She turns to Tannan. "With someone who knows how to program, it can be used as a means to bypass some of the security in the Inner Circle and probably the Palace."

"Will it get them into Virreal?"

She raises an eyebrow. "You're going to Virreal? Wow, I knew you were brave, Tye." She shakes her head. "The things you do for those in need. I don't know if the Faithful can ever thank you for all you've done for us." She sighs, then turns back to Hart's tablet. "Obviously, the interface itself can't be a direct link; you'll need to access a unit, but if you jack the interface in, it can be used to bypass certain security aspects; again, only if you know how to write the program."

Tannan frowns. "Do you–" Lyris is shaking her head before he can even ask.

"Sorry, but no. I'm good with the mechanics but the interior is beyond my wheelhouse. I haven't had an opportunity to learn the inner workings. Never allowed close enough to the Inner Circle to interact with an interface like this." She grins. "Actually, that's why I was so excited to get my hands on him." She takes the console off Tye again and begins flicking through settings and operating commands in the user interface. "I was looking forward to exploring."

I shudder at the idea and hold my hand out for the tablet. "Please don't mess with it. I need him to be Hart when you bring him back online." Lyris sighs and hands the console to me. I browse through the settings and sigh with relief to find the system is both fully functional and unrestricted. Even the code has hints of the strange way Hart talks. The text on the screen is like a familiar friend. Hart is still in here. We can get him back.

"Can you work it?" Tye asks. I nod.

"Yes." I reach over and dig through some of the debris of Hart's parts on the table until I pull free a cable. "I don't know if this will link with your systems. It's the same cable hook-up we use on Elixr."

Lyris checks the ends of the cord. "The City of Light was constructed from the same technologies as your starship so it's possible those mechanics will work." She reaches behind her and digs through a tray of parts on another desk. After a short rustle, she pulls out some other parts. "But if you run into any problems, try these." She takes the wires, and a wire stripper, strips the ends of each of the cords. I gasp and she smiles. Then she connects additional port sockets and creates an adaptable connection to the end of the cord in a matter of deccas.

I raise an eyebrow. "Adaptors?"

She nods. "Yes. See, now you can plug and unplug each connection so if you run into troubles with the ports, you can switch out for the kind you need. The Virreal unit in particular is more likely to use this one rather than that. It's newer tech, post-Shadow."

I nod, only understanding half of what she is saying but understanding enough that I'm sure I'll be able to use the device effectively.

Tannan taps the table. "What about the creds you were going to secure? For the Inner Circle?"

"Right," Lyris says, she turns to a console against one wall of the lab and pulls up a schematic. "This pass will get you past the Outer Circle no problem, but you'll need better creds to access some parts of the Inner Circle and the Palace itself." A loud buzz whirrs around us as the machine prints. I watch as a couple of small chip cards with holo-IDs on them materialise. It's a lot like the fabricator on the Elixr but seems to be more manual based, drawing from a tray of glass rather than a fabrication drive for raw components.

"Just two?" Tye asks.

"That's all I could source codes for. I mean I could print duplicates but the odds of it triggering an alert increase significantly. How many did you need?"

Tannan shakes his head. "Two will have to do." I feel suddenly nervous, knowing that Tye and I will have to go into the city alone. I swallow and bite my lip.

Tye takes both creds from Lyris and hands one to me. It's still warm from the printing process. I glance down at it, surprised to see my likeness. It's not me of course, it's Bellamy, and I remember then that part of this depends on me entering the city with a face that isn't really mine.

Tye glances back at Hart's array of parts. "When we get back with the girl–"

"Wish."

He nods. "Yes, when we get back with Wish, we'll need him functional." Tye turns to me. "You need him to make the cure work, right?"

I dip my chin. It's not strictly true, at least I don't think so. But if Lyris can fix his memory systems I'll know more. "I need him," I say, choosing not to state a full truth but instead, a half one.

Tye smiles and it's reassuring to know he's on my side. He turns to Lyris. "She needs him functional by the time we get back."

Lyris grins and offers him a mock salute. "No problem. Blake and Jenin will be back with parts soon and he's all I'll work on until he's fully restored."

Tannan nods. "That's good to hear."

Tye turns to me. "Looks like we're headed up to the city." His eyes sparkle with excitement for the adventure ahead and he grins. "You ain't seen nothing yet," he says with a wink.

19

Trust Goes Both Ways

Wish

The cell is exactly seventeen steps by fourteen. I pace the edges of it at least twenty-two times before I settle against a wall. I take one look at the small ragged bed and decide even the chilly tiles would be better for my health than that flea-riddled tick-trap. I'd slept, I think. As another few deccas tick past, I wonder exactly how many factors I've been here. Should I give up waiting for Niah and try to escape?

I glance up at the small window. I spent quite a few of those factors gazing out at the city below. This vantage point, in what must be a high tower in a replica of the Lord's Palace, reveals a whole world below me. Even far beyond the reach of the city's life-sustaining dome, I can see trees, rolling hills, even distant mountains and what is either a large lake or the edge of an ocean. My mind struggles to comprehend the vastness so it's comforting to retreat within the four barren walls.

"Too high, and I don't think it's real anyway," I mutter to myself.

"It's not."

I startle, shocked by the voice in my cell. I glance around and spot a young boy sitting on the bed. I look around the room again, wondering where he might have come from. I can't believe I never noticed him in all the steps I've taken around this space. He's younger than me, probably only eight or nine narcycles.

"Where did you come from?"

He shrugs. "The City of Light." I blink, because isn't that where we are?

"How did you get here?"

"Virreal. Muma says I shouldn't stray the programs but I didn'a want to be a pirate swabby or echo thief again. I ain't strong 'nough to play fisban with Jordie and Simon. 'Sides, I like the Palace. I like Oli's puppy."

"What do you mean?"

"Lord Oliver calls her Chortessa. She eats people, but she doesn't eat me. She's my friend."

"She is? But she's a beast."

A sadness darkens his eyes. "No she ain't. She's just a puppy. The Lord ain't nice to her but she's not mean. She's my friend."

I nod, pushing myself to my feet. I move across the room and brave the fleas to sit down beside him. "You don't have many of those?"

He shakes his head. "Nah. Muma says it's 'cause we don't belong to the Inner Circle. So, they shoe, um, nah they shun? I think that's it, they shuns us." His head drops and he rocks in place. "That's why I stray the programs sometimes, 'cause I don't fit in like the other kids."

"What does that mean? About the programs?"

He lifts his head with a look of surprise. "You don't know 'bout the programs? But you're in Virreal too. How'd you get here if you don't know 'bout 'em?"

I shrug. "A man brought me. They plugged my mind into the machine."

His mouth drops open. "So you ain't even pick your own program?" He glances around. "I guess that 'splains why you is here. Pretty boring program."

I glance around too. "Yeah, it is."

"Want to see something else?"

I look back at him, startled. "I don't think I can. They locked me in the cell."

He blinks. "But it's just a program."

I know my confusion must be marked all over my face. He sighs.

"You don't know nothing do you? Virreal ain't real. You can change the program, go somewhere else."

"I don't know how to do that."

His brow furrows for a moment. His eyes seem to go distant before he snaps back to attention with a look of determination. He smiles. "Wanna come with me?"

"Where will we go? Can we find my sister?"

"Is she in Virreal?"

"I don't know." I frown, realising that I have no idea where Niah is now. I'd felt so sure she must be coming for me but maybe she's as trapped as I am.

Maybe she needs me to rescue her. "Maybe we can find out? Maybe we can rescue her." I smile at the boy.

He grins. "Like a real adventure?"

I nod. "Yeah, an adventure. If we can escape this place, we can find out where she is, and we can save her. Are you with me?"

"Sure!" He pushes himself up from the bed and pats his hands down the thighs of his pants as if dusting himself off, but his dress pants and fine shirt are immaculate.

I stand too and then turn back to him. "I'm Wish by the way," I say, giving him my hand.

He smiles up at me and takes my hand. "My name's Casper." Our hands remain linked as he closes his eyes and turns to face the cell door. I watch the sneaky smile on his face before he opens his eyes. And in the breath before I can ask him what he's doing, I hear the heavy clunk of the cell door unlocking. The door springs open of its own accord and beyond it, we can see an empty, abandoned hallway.

I smile, hopeful and excited. Maybe we really can save Niah. Maybe we can save all of Nar.

Niah

The catacombs of the City Below are a honeycomb maze of networking corridors and chambers. Even this upper level, which must be near the surface, seems to wander. I stay close to Tye's side. I'm glad for the escort because I don't know that I'd ever find the way out on my own. The darker corridors create a more pit-like sense of claustrophobia around me. Perhaps it's also the layer of smoke that seems to blanket the City Below. The faces we see as we move through the halls are ash-stained. Some of the Faithful appear sickly and frail.

"How many people live down here?" I ask as we pass an eating hall with long tables and benches that could seat dozens of families.

Tye shrugs. "I don't know about permanent residents but I've seen that hall to capacity when all the Shadows come in for a meeting, or to escape a bluster storm or dark moon."

I don't know what either of those things are but I guess, unless I'm stuck outside during either, I probably don't need to know. We round another corner and enter a small chamber lit from above by a slatted window of stained glass. A heavy metal step ladder rises up to a trapdoor in the ceiling.

"Want to go first?" Tye asks.

I shake my head, not sure what we'll find above us. "I'll follow you."

He nods and begins climbing. As he reaches the trapdoor, he nudges it aside. It opens easily and tips with a clunk up onto the floor above us. He climbs through, then turns to reach down and help me up.

As I pull up through the door and stand within the small antechamber, I'm amazed at the difference between the barren darkness of the City Below and the charming beauty and pearlescent softness of the carefully crafted walls, the decorative stained-glass windows that cast a rainbow of light around the room, and the fixtures of finely carved furniture. The open door looks out on a large room arrayed in worship pews, a draped altar, and beautiful stone monuments.

"It's a church?" I ask.

"Chapel of the Faithful."

"You openly worship Bellamy on the surface?"

Tye shakes his head. "Not overtly. The front is a place of worship for the Lord actually." He grins and I laugh.

"He must have some ego."

"Oh, yeah. Of course, there are other purposes for the chapels. It's considered non-denominational so those who worship the Sacred of Nar, or the Universal Void, or even the Elixir of the Gods will worship at our chapels. Even share ceremonies some of the time. But almost every Chapel of the Faithful is an access point to the City Below. There are several in the Outer Circle."

"What about the Inner Circle?"

He sighs. "There are chapels there but the City Below doesn't run under the central towers. The Lord's tech penetrates under several levels into the basins where his most top-secret research is conducted."

"How do you know all this?"

He smiles. "The Faithful have spent two hundred narcycles developing the society and the city formed up around them. We Shadows don't only stalk the Shadowland."

I frown. "Why do you call yourself a Shadow?"

He sighs. "That's what I am. My family have been outcast for generations. It's so long ago now that only the Lord would know why, but it means I have no place in the City of Light. I couldn't bear the confinement of the City Below either, so when I was about seven, Tannan started to let me venture out with the Shadows. We're trawlers and herders and explorers. There's a whole world beyond the edges of the Outer Rim and while it currently lies in the shadows, we shouldn't ever forget that it's out there."

I nod.

"Come on," he says, "this is just the first stop. We're on an outskirt of the Outer Circle and there's a checkpoint to the north, but we have to move through the city to get there. To do that, we need to look the part."

Tye leads the way through the chapel and out a door at the back of the great hall. It leads into a narrow alley stretching between the high walls of the chapel and a row of what looks like residential apartments. Above us, the strange sky is lit up by a brilliant, almost blinding radiance. I gaze up at it, wondering how the light is created. The Shadowlands seemed like an eternal night, so the sight of twin suns feels oddly unnatural.

"The caretaker's cottage is at the end of this row. The Faithful keep supplies there. No staples, they're too valuable to leave unattended, but plenty of fresh clothes and hot water." Tye pauses, then says, "The dome has an artificial sky." I look down to see him watching me with a raised eyebrow. He chuckles. "The Lord likes to be extravagant." I smile. "Come on."

He grabs my hand and we jog together down the row to a small rise of stone columns and fibreglass panels. He nudges open the heavy door. Lights flicker on as we step into the room. "Welcome," says a soft female voice. "Please be considerate in your stay."

The disembodied voice is so familiar that it's eerie. "She reminds me of Elixr," I say. I glance around. The rest of the room is familiar too. Its walls are made from the same white fibreglass and chrome. The high technology is a startling contrast to the earthen walls and dark wood furnishings in the City Below.

"Your ship?" Tye asks. I can feel his eyes on me as I explore the room. Each element of decor is clean and functional, minimalist. It looks pristine, unused, unlived in.

I nod as I run my hand across the smooth white leather sofa. "Yes, she has a voice interface like this one." I smile. "White is a fashion trend there, too."

Tye shakes his head. "The welcome bot isn't really an interface. It's programmed to deliver the message but doesn't listen for commands. We have our privacy here. But we shouldn't stay long; the later we leave things, the more Stalkers will be on the streets when we try to cross into the Inner Circle. I don't want to draw attention to you. Your features are a little too distinct to pass for an average Narian."

I sigh, because again Captain Bellamy's face is haunting me. Tye shows me to a room with a closet of Narian clothing and an attached bathroom with jettison shower. It's odd to see a cascade of real water streaming from the pipes above rather than the starship's waterless particle cleanser.

I can't help lingering in the shower a little but change back into my clothes quickly. I pull a set of Narian clothing over my suit. Then, seeing a satchel in the closet, I take that and drop it over my shoulder. I tuck Hart's tablet inside.

Tye is faster. He's waiting as I return to the main room. Seeing him clean-faced with a golden mop of hair gives me an odd rush of wanting. I bite down on the inside of my lip. His eyes seem to devour me, mirroring my yearning, and I wonder what's different. I suppose it's the clothes.

"Do I look okay?" I ask, crunching the edge of the dark shirt in my fingers.

"Depends," he says. His Adam's apple bobs as he swallows, then looks me up and down again. "Will you be offended if I say I see Bellamy in you?"

I sigh. "I suppose not. That's kind of what we're going for, right?"

He smiles and then hands me a black mamot cloak with a fitted hood. "In part, but not always. Here. While we move through the more populated parts of the city, you should keep this on. We don't know who will be friendly to our cause, and seeing your features might draw more attention than necessary."

I nod and pull the cloak around my shoulders. I pull the hood up over my hair and let the lip hang low over my eyes.

"Perfect, now you could pass for a Stalker."

I smile. "And you? You don't look anything like Hanzor or Erron."

He grins. "Well, some Stalkers can be charming." He winks and I laugh.

"Is that what you are?" I raise an eyebrow at him and he laughs too.

"Just go with it. I'll pass. Besides, we have creds to get us past the first boundary so we shouldn't have any problems with that."

"Let's go then!"

20

Streets Within Streets

Niah

"Okay," Tye says, "follow my lead; the crossing isn't far. Hood up, remember."

I tuck the hood close so that even a stray breeze couldn't tug it away and follow Tye as he exits through the front door. He secures it behind me before turning out onto the street.

It's busier now. The streets are lined with residences giving way to commercial buildings. People bustle about their business. On a nearby street corner a tired looking shop keeper haggles with a harried mother. A young man steps into a store with scrolling advertising running down its fronting windows. In pairs, or small groups, people dart across the road, zigzagging through traffic. I step aside as a narrow, slipstream vehicle zips past. The solar panels across its surface reflect the light from the artificial suns.

I glance up, realising the suns are high now. The circuit is passing. I worry about Wish and the deadline but Tye moves ahead as if everything is going to plan.

As we reach a boundary, Tye lifts his head even higher. He strides forward with confidence, as if he makes the crossing every single circuit. I watch how he presses the credential through the device. It chimes, giving a tinkling ping. He moves through the unit and continues walking.

I try to follow his lead. I'm less confident and perhaps more conspicuous because of it. I fumble with the card and it drops from my fingers to the floor. "Oh, sorry." I say, then remember I'm trying to pass for a man. I clear my throat as I crouch to pick up the card. I slam it through the sensor and then rush through the unit.

Tye's steps have slowed almost imperceptibly but he keeps walking as I catch up just behind him. The Stalkers at the border barely acknowledge us. We move past them, into the street beyond, and I breathe a sigh of relief.

Tye throws me a sidelong look. He raises a cheeky eyebrow. "Fun, hey? Wanna do it again?"

I chuckle, feeling the tension leave my shoulders. "Not any time soon. First hurdle's the hardest, right?"

He laughs at that. "Hardly. But we can do this."

We weave through the crowds gathered in the streets that lead through the Inner Circle. There appears to be some kind of market stall here. Vendors sell everything from foods I've never heard of to games and plants. All of it significantly more extravagant than in the Outer Circle.

The people are more extravagant, too, dressed in

fine silk and lace that has been cut and sewn to fit their slender frames. Their hair and faces are impeccably made up and every person seems completely in their element, in their place, as if they each belong. By contrast, I feel like an imposter, lingering in the shadows, portraying myself as one thing when really I'm another.

The streets continue in a weave that crisscrosses the city. Tye keeps moving steadily toward the Palace in the distance.

As we move away from the looming walls that divide the Inner and Outer Circles, the tablet I tucked into the satchel at my side begins to bleep. I glance around, alarmed that we might be noticed by the odd noise. A couple of people glance up but their interest swiftly fades. I pull out the tablet and glance down at the screen.

After flipping through several settings, I work out that the device seems to be recording some strange details, but it's coded in a language I've not seen before. I pause under the shingle of a nearby building and try to decipher the scripts that are running. The dimensional plane of the code feels wonky and I wonder if perhaps it has something to do with the curving plane of the planet's surface or the dome above us. The telemetry unit is definitely running some sort of diagnostics and statistical imaging but I'm not sure exactly what the data represents.

I sigh, giving up on making sense of it right now, and tuck the tablet back into the satchel. I glance around for Tye. My heart sinks and my chest tightens when I realise he's nowhere in sight. I dash forward through the streets, trying to catch up, but still can't find him.

"Tye?" I call out. A handful of people gaze at me and I drop my chin, hiding my face from their curious glances. "Eagrim's beak, now what do I do?"

Tye

"Niah?" I shout again. I must have wandered and backtracked for at least a factor or two but still can't find her. I kick at a discarded bottle in the street when I really wish I could kick myself. "How in the nine-voids could I lose her?" I mutter to myself, then grimace. "Niah!" I shout again.

I gaze around. The few people remaining in the streets give me an odd look. It's not normal for someone to be shouting here. All of the adventure happens in Virreal, so circuit-to-circuit life in the Inner Circle is relatively dull. In the solar, that is; at night it's a different story. I give a wary glance at the solars, which are swiftly diving for the horizon.

While the Outer Circle is full of hard working men and women who go home to sleep after dark, lights out in the Inner Circle brings out the troubled and the defiant. With too many staples to lead sensible lives, they splurge on warraroot, a powerful opiate that warps their minds, or spend too many factors sipping tallow nectar at the nectar bars and casinos along the wealth strip.

The Lord seems to like it this way. Shrouded and protected as he is in his Palace, he escapes into Virreal more often than not for a greater than reality experience himself. He reaps the staples of the Inner Circle and Virreal keeps them tethered to the cycles of the City of Light like batteries wired into a circuit.

All this to say that after lights out the fringes of the Inner Circle are no place to be, especially for an otherworlder so totally out of her element. I dash back down the way I came, wondering again how we'd become separated. If she returned to where we parted ways, I might find her by retracing our path. I was in sight of the checkpoint when I realised she was no longer following.

"Niah?" I call. I ignore the suspicious looks the checkpoint Stalkers give me. They mutter to each other, and when one leans down to murmur something to the other, I decide ignorance probably won't help me as effectively as inebriation. So, I act drunk, or high, or both and give them a cheery ahoy before promptly stumbling over my own feet and then laughing about it like a loon. The Stalkers wave off and I breathe a sigh of relief before ducking down an alley out of sight.

I glance around, wondering where she might have wandered. I grow more and more frustrated when each turn fails to reveal her. How could I have been so stupid? I should have kept her closer beside me. I should have paid more attention. The weight in the pit of my gut keeps growing. If anything happens to her…

I shake my head, forcing out the worst thoughts. "No," I mutter to myself, feeling confidence in hearing my own voice. "I'll find her. She's here, somewhere."

Niah

Determined to catch up with Tye and to find Wish, I keep moving toward the Palace rather than away from it. The high walls rise up in the distance several blocks away. As I round a final corner, the whole building spreads out before me. It looms tall with turrets and floors reaching above the nearby buildings. A huge white wall separates the elite from the rest of the Inner Circle.

Outside the inner bailey, a young girl lingers with a small pot in her hands. Her face is dirty and her clothes haggard which, in this part of the city, stands out so completely that I'm curious. I move toward her but a bustle of people near the gates becomes rowdy. The girl darts away from the rabble like a startled rabbit.

A man strides across the courtyard. He turns to shout a command to another man across the way and slams into me. He wears a long black cloak like the one Tye gave me. "Hey!" He snarls at me as if my being there were the cause of the accident rather than his careless step.

"I'm sorry." I don't know why I apologise, perhaps it's the judgement in his eyes or the superiority in his stance.

He grits his teeth and nods but as I go to move past him he shakes his head. "Where you going, moon-skitter?"

I glance to where the girl was standing but she's nowhere in sight.

"Back in line!" the man snaps. It's a command more than a suggestion. He waves to the queue of dark cloaked men who are gathered in formation, then marches to a raised platform overlooking them all. "Listen up, Men!"

The men around me snap to attention like an armed force. I realise then that they're all wearing cloaks like mine. Tye said I was supposed to blend in like a Stalker. Like these Stalkers? I don't want to draw their attention. I don't want to ask for their help. They move with dark determination and the expressions on their faces are far from welcoming. The swift disappearance of any remaining Inner Circle residents is also a bad sign. I follow their movements and try not to draw attention to myself.

I keep my head down, trying to blend in among the ranks of men. The commander yells at the troops for a time but I don't understand most of what he's telling them. Something about shifts and quota. As he falls silent, glaring at the men with a harsh rebuke, the tablet in my satchel bleeps in chaotic frenzy.

Dozens of eyes turn on me, including the dark glare of the commander. I want to crawl into a hole and hide but there's no way to escape their attention. The white line of fury marring the commander's lip is the most daunting of all.

"Stand front!" he shouts.

I pretend he isn't shouting at me and fumble a hand in my satchel, trying to figure out how to mute the tablet without taking it out of the bag.

"Men, seize him!"

I spin, preparing to run, but three set of hands

clamp down on my arms. They march me forward and drop me at the foot of the commander. Part of me wants to lift my head to glare at him, the rest of me remembers that I wear Bellamy's face, and right now, being Bellamy could be a death sentence.

I swallow and glance up when the blips of alarm from the tablet stop. The commander's gaze is fixed on me.

"What's your name, Stalker?"

I bite my lip, not sure how to respond. Then I remember the credential Lyris gave me. I pull it out of my satchel and hand it up to him. He snatches it from me with a snarl.

I hear his gasp and then remember. The cred has Bellamy's actual face printed in holographic technicolour. And I was afraid to show my own face for fear they'd mistake me for Bellamy. How stupid could I be? I turn, dart under the hands of the nearby Stalkers, and run for the nearest shadow I can find.

21

Programs Within Programs

Wish

"Where are the guards?"

Casper turns to me and winks. "This is our program. Do ya want guards? I can put 'em back."

I grin. "Actually, no guards is good. So how do we find my sister?"

Casper's forehead wrinkles in a furrow as he thinks about the question. "If she ain't in Virreal then we ain't gonna find her here."

"I don't know. What if she is?"

"Maybe we should check the other cells."

He walks down the corridor and rests his hand on the next cell door. It clanks as it unlocks and then swings open. We step in and look around but it's empty. We continue this way down several cells until the last. I startle as a hand grips my arm and spins me into a lock hold with my back slammed against a thick chest. I gasp and another hand slams over my mouth.

"Don't scream, don't say a word," a rough voice

whispers in my ear. I shiver at the feel of his breath sliding down my neck. I try to pull away but his arms tighten around me.

"Hey, you're not supposed to be here," Casper says. "It's not your program."

My captor turns us to face the boy and Casper shrinks back. His mouth drops open in shock. "What do you know about it, kid?"

"You're– you– but you're," Casper's words stumble out of him.

"No I ain't. I just look like him. What do you know about the programs?"

I try to shake my head but he's gripping me so tight that I can barely move.

"Let her go! She's my friend."

The man ignores him and my stomach tenses as I wonder what this man could possibly want. I push my head back, trying to see his face. He adds more pressure to my arm and I wince in pain but push against it to see him. His face is dark with a shadow of stubble and filth. His mottled hair is shaggy and unkempt. Everything about him seems abandoned and bereft. Except for his eyes. There's something in his eyes as they glimmer in the shadows. He reminds me of Niah.

"Tell me about the programs."

Casper's eyes fix on me. "Captain Bellamy," the boy pleads, "please let her go. You're hurting her."

The man looks down on me and I see a hint of compassion in his eyes before it disappears behind a mask of steel. But he loosens his grip slightly and mutters, "You're not going to scream?"

I shake my head. He lifts his hand away but steps

between us and the door as he lets me go.

"You're Captain Bellamy? We thought you died. On the Elixr."

Casper's hurt gaze turns on me. "B– B–," he begins. He sucks a breath into his chest then finishes in a gasp. "Bellamy died?"

I reach a hand out and place it on his shoulder. "Hey, it's okay. Look, he's right there, see?"

Casper blinks, glancing at the Bellamy that seems tangible, real, and very much alive in front of us. Casper's bottom lip wobbles and I can see his sharp mind processing the details. "But he's part of the program."

"Aren't we all part of the program? That's how VR works right? We're plugged into the machine."

He glances between me and Bellamy. "I guess. Are you come to save Nar, Mr. Bellamy?"

Bellamy grimaces and chuckles. It sounds dark and hopeless. "Save Nar? I can never save Nar. No matter how many times I try and I've been trying every circuit of my life."

I furrow my brow at that because his voice is gritty, as if he's lived for more circuits than his face would have us believe. Casper's wide eyes gaze up at him. "But you have to! That's what they always said."

"Who said?"

Casper leans forward and whispers with a small voice that echoes around the room, "The Faithful."

Bellamy shakes his head. "Never heard of them."

"Well, I'm not s'posed to know. Muma says I'm not s'posed to talk to Tye and the others but him's a good friend. He likes to hear 'bout where I go in

Virreal. I don't tell the others 'cause they might tell Muma but Tye never would. He tells me about the Shadowlands and I tell him about Virreal. He's my friend."

"Not heard of him either, buddy."

"That's why I know you're gonna save us. You went on a big ship and flied away a long, long time ago. Now you're back, you're gonna deliver the cure."

Bellamy sighs and turns away. He stalks across the room and gazes out of the tempered glass. I glance at the door. He's left a clear path so Casper and I could make a run for it right now, but for some reason I don't. Instead, I turn to him. "You could help us."

He glances back at me. His eyes show a soul-heavy weariness. "You have the face of my brother." I shiver at the emptiness in his voice when he says those words. I can't imagine ever feeling so torn to pieces at the idea of seeing Niah in someone else's face. Although it is eerie seeing hints of her in his.

"I see my sister in you."

He swallows hard then nods. "Programs?"

I shake my head. "We came on the Elixr."

He blinks and I watch the thoughts tick through his mind before his mouth drops open on a whisper. "Clones?"

I nod.

"Then maybe there is hope."

Tye

The streets become more and more deserted. It gets harder to know where Niah might be because in place of the Inner Circle's citizens march several groups of Stalkers. All of them wear black mamot cloaks. The exact kind I'd given Niah, and wear myself, so that we might pass for Stalkers and gain access to parts of the outer courtyard of the Palace without notice.

I glance around, searching the raised hoods for Niah's face. The men move with sure steps and confident strides. I don't hold much hope that she's among them, but with no other leads and a growing sense of danger I try to find her among the sea of black.

When I can't find her, I fall into step behind two Stalkers headed in the same direction as the others. Shouting in the distance sets the two men racing forward. I give chase, just another concerned Stalker racing toward a dispute that needs settling.

"Seize him! It's Bellamy! Stop him!"

I gasp, my gaze drawn to a small figure darting between a forest of leathery cloaks. Beneath the hood, I see a glimpse of her pale hair and the gleam of her eyes. "Niah," I whisper, then take in the chaos around her.

Behind her, the High Commander is ordering troops with one hand and reaching for his weapon with the other. "Men, close ranks!" he barks. The Stalkers around Niah stumble as they sluggishly move to obey the command. The Inner Circle guards rarely face true conflict. Most spend a half ration of every circuit inside Virreal, so their physical reflexes are clumsy.

Niah races forward, streaking between the arms and legs of the swirl of guards. Nimble and quick. I can see the flush in her face. Her chest rises and falls as she strains for breath. My own breath catches as I worry about how her health will fare against the exertion and how I can possibly help her escape.

The High Commander levels his plasma pulse rifle. His finger tightens around the trigger. My heart jumps. Everything seems to move in slow motion and yet too fast. There's too much distance between me and the High Commander, between me and Niah, between me and any sort of effective intervention. The weapon fires and a burst of white hot plasma spears forward like a blast of electricity.

"Niah!" The word leaves my throat before I even realise I've spoken. Her eyes meet mine as the searing energy slams into her back. A shimmer of green pulses around her in an orb. She slams to the ground as if hit, but the burst of plasma splatters out from a point inches behind her. "What the void?" I almost stumble in shock but press myself forward, racing to her side.

Niah

I slam into the ground hard. The wind bursts from my lungs. I gasp for breath and glance up as a hand reaches down to me. Tye. I grab his hand and he pulls me to my feet.

We scramble down the nearest alley and dart from door to door until Tye bursts through an unlocked portal, startling the residents sitting down to dinner.

"What was that?" I ask.

"I was going to ask you the same thing." He glances behind me. "There's no time. We've got to get out of here!"

"Sorry!" he shouts, sprinting through their living space and out through the rear exit. I race just steps behind him.

The people are angered by the intrusion, but when they see my face they prostrate themselves and bow their heads muttering, "Bellamy." I grimace, pulling the hood of the cloak tighter around me as I sprint to keep pace with Tye.

We weave through several alleys. Behind me, I can hear the Stalkers gaining ground as I lose momentum. I curse the weight in my limbs and the tightness in my lungs. I swallow the rise of vomit at the back of my throat and bite down on my lip to distract myself from the swirling heave of my stomach.

"Tye!" I call out. My voice is tight and quieter than I expected but he glances back and slows his pace. His face is wreathed in worry.

"I'm sorry Niah, we can't stop. Can you go just a little farther?"

I drag a breath into my aching lungs. "I don't think I can." I glance back and see the Stalkers approaching. The nearest raises a weapon. The flash of the plasma pulse shocks me. It lances through the air so fast I barely have a chance to take a breath, let alone react, before it's just inches from my chest.

The pulse of green energy bursts up around me

again. It's an imperfect orb, emanating from my right hip rather than my centre, but I'd never seen anything like it. Well, except for the warp shield on the Elixr.

The pulse blast scatters off the edges of the strange orb of energy. Tye grabs my hand and drags me into the shelter of another alley. "It's here! We're so close, Niah! Just a little farther." He weaves through another twisting maze of turns, then slows and inspects a wall in the fading light. He stops, pressing a small marking carved almost imperceptibly into the stonework of the wall. The section slides open, revealing a tight corridor of stone and metal.

Tye glances back at the Stalkers rounding the corner, then turns to me. "You have to go in. Quick Niah, hide."

I step into the corridor and Tye slams the strange button. As the heavy door slides back into place I catch a glimpse of Tye taking a swing at the first Stalker to come in reach. He kicks away the man's plasma pulser. The weapon skates across the floor toward me, but the door slams into place before I can reach for it.

22

Mazes Within Mazes

Niah

I stare at the solid darkness in front of me. Tye is trapped with a dozen Stalkers on the other side. I slam my fists in the door trying to make it open again. "Tye!" I scream. "Tye!"

On this side, the wall is smooth. Even the sounds from the street are muted by the wall between us.

"Tye?" I cry again, hammering the wall until my arms ache. I lean my head against the wall and try to imagine him surviving. Are they hauling him away? Is he lying on the ground, vicious lances of seared flesh torn through him by their plasma weapons? A tear strays down my cheek.

I rest my head against the cold wall. My breath slows as minutes pass. Eventually, I suck a breath into my lungs and force myself to push away from the wall. I glance around. The darkness is pitch.

I try to remember the shape of this corridor, the directions and lines. I bite my lip, then remember the glowing blue screen of Hart's interface. I reach down to pull the device from the satchel that's still sitting against my hip. The screen lights up, casting a soft blue glow around me. The light bounces off the smooth chrome walls.

The odd text still scrolls. Amongst the data from the recent stream I recognise some symbols. They remind me of the interior bitdata language I've seen in Elixr's base command. "Shield?" I gaze at the device, then at my hip. "No!"

I scroll back through the text and see the word again. Beside it, is the strange jumble of non-dimensional data. I gasp, realising why I can't understand the linear design of the data. I sit down with my back against the wall and bury myself in the code, typing in new commands to create a user interface that more accurately represents the information streaming through the telemetry sensors of the device.

As I execute the final command, I smile and watch the stream of strange words and commands as it scatters and staggers into a three-dimensional representation of the city in multiple layers. Icons and images drop into place. Among the glowing dots scrawled across the screen, I notice one marked with a special symbol. "What is that?"

I zoom the screen to look at the icon more closely. It's the same logo that marked the Elixr. I narrow my gaze then zoom out again, examining the surrounding area and the unmoving dot. "No!" I gasp. I stand and start walking along the channel of the chamber. The dot begins moving.

I freeze and run my gaze over the other dots on the screen, searching and searching until I see it.

Far to the north, at least three furlongs, is an echo of my own dot. Barely moving, confined to what looks like a large room, and vastly, significantly, alone.

"Wish!" I pull back the map and scan for a route. The strange caverns between the buildings and below the city wind like a maze, but among the twists and turns is a way to reach her. "I'm coming, Wish. I'm coming."

I hold the tablet close and walk down the corridor, following the winding twists. My head pounds and I use the wall to steady myself. I pause to check the device regularly and as I get closer and closer to Wish, I feel a small burst of energy. My body is exhausted, but every breath of my being strains to reach her. So, I keep pushing onward.

Wish

The room around us flickers as if the walls are made of the iridescent flames of a blue giant. The hopeful spark that flashed in Bellamy's eyes fades and he closes his eyes. "You should both go if you can. He is coming."

"What do you mean?"

"GO!" He shouts.

I grab Casper's hand and we dash to the door but it's too late. The door flies off its hinges. I freeze in place, face to face with my doppelgänger. "Oliver," I whisper. His eyes narrow and he glares at me.

Beside me Casper hisses. "It's LORD Oliver, Wish." I swallow, realising my mistake.

The Lord strolls into the room. He pats Casper

on the shoulder as he passes between us and moves to stand, making a square with equal distance between the three of us. "Well, well, what have we got here? I don't recall permitting you to have visitors, Brother."

Bellamy scowls but says nothing. Lord Oliver turns to look at him. He fixes a gaze on him so glowering that I shiver. Bellamy swallows. "They came upon me. I had nothing to do with it."

My jaw drops at his betrayal. There's so much of Niah in him that my heart aches as if she betrayed me herself. A part of me knows his words are the truth, but knowing it doesn't stop the pain.

"Indeed?" The Lord raises an eyebrow and looks at me.

I drop my eyes, not sure how to respond. Then, growing angry at my own lack of response, I lift my chin and glare back at him. "Where is my sister?"

He lifts his hand to his chin. "Sister?"

I flinch, realising Lord Oliver still doesn't know that the person they mistook for the real Captain Bellamy is actually Niah. I swallow back the swell of fear in my throat.

"Come now, child. I would gladly help you find your sister. If you know where she might be, we could perhaps both be reunited with our siblings."

I shake my head. "I don't know where she is."

His gaze narrows. "No, I suppose you don't." He pauses, paces the room and then turns back to me. "But you do know something about the ship, don't you?"

The Bellamy beside me grimaces, then says,

"Leave her alone, Oli. She's just a kid."

Lord Oliver swings toward him and Bellamy flinches back as if afraid to be struck. My heart aches at what must have become a conditioned response. Bellamy never seemed to be so spineless in the Elixr's recordings of him. Maybe that Bellamy was changed from his narcycles is space, but surely a captain that could jettison himself and his crew for his home world, was built with a courageous soul. How had this Bellamy become a shadow of that?

With a snarl, the Lord lifts a hand, forming a fist. Bellamy drops to his knees. He raises his arms, as if trying to shield himself from a crushing pain, and whimpers. Lord Oliver's hand relaxes and Bellamy's shoulders droop. Tears streak down his murky cheeks.

"Did you say something, Brother?" Lord Oliver asks. His voice is quiet with a cutting edge of volatile rage. My breath catches, instinctively stilling to avoid setting off the violent explosion of his anger. "Do I not have the right to ask a simple question in my own Palace? In my own world?" He raises his hands as if inviting us to admire the wonder of his creation. Around us, the walls, floor, and ceiling flicker through a thousand settings. Vast mountain ranges, sprawling oceans, flower-studded fields, crystal temples, vibrantly alive rainforests, and a thousand other sights, both Nar and beyond. Some include hints of scenes I remember from my before thoughts, as if they were shaped in my dreams. My mouth drops open.

Beside me, Casper reaches out as if to touch the

lands flashing by around him. "Wow, Mis– I mean, Lord Oliver. You have so many programs!"

I reach up to capture Casper's hand and bring it close to me instead. I step in front of him to prevent the Lord from fixing his eyes on the boy. The edge of the Lord's lip tips up as he observes my movement.

He steps around me and takes Casper's hand from mine. "Hello there, and who might you be?"

Casper blinks up at him, eyes wide with awe. "Me, sir? I'm Casper." Casper steps forward, close to Lord Oliver's ear, he leans in and whispers. "I'm not supposed to be here."

The change in the Lord's features is radiant as he gives his first genuine smile. "Is that so?"

Casper shakes his head. "But I wanted to come visit the Palace. Muma said I'm not s'posed to, that I'm aposta only do the study levels. But I done them already and I wanted to see the Palace. 'Sides," he whispers again, "I'm gonna visit your puppy."

"Really? You're a charming young man." Lord Oliver lifts his eyes to mine. "Don't you think?"

I square my chin and meet the Lord's fixed gaze but say nothing.

The breath bursts from my lips as a sting of pain radiates from my cheek, through the bones of my jaw, and up to my eyes. I blink back tears. My hand lifts to my stinging cheek and I glare at the man who delivered the bruising blow.

Bellamy steps forward but the Lord raises a hand at him and he freezes in place. Lord Oliver's eyes, still fixed on mine, narrow on me with a stark, brutal scowl. "Dare you defy me?"

I bite my lip and shake my head. Lord Oliver snarls and spins on his foot to pace the cell. When he turns, he fixes a gaze first on Bellamy, then on me, and back again.

"What am I going to do with you both?"

When neither of us venture a word, the Lord's lips curve up in a smile.

"Perhaps you all would like to play with Chortessa. I did say your friends would have more time, but I assume they don't intend to deliver Jacob to me, so is there really any harm in changing the timeline? Besides, I'm sure I could encourage Chortessa to take her time with you. Four factors in the pit might loosen your tongue."

I swallow, remembering the vicious beast he called Chortessa. I glance at Casper; he's smiling too.

"Puppy? Can I go too?"

Lord Oliver tilts his head and looks down on the boy as he considers the request. "I suppose you can. Come then."

The Lord clicks his fingers and the room around us shimmers and changes again. This time, Bellamy, Casper, and I stand together in an open-skied corridor that seems to stretch endlessly in either direction. I frown, looking first one way then the other. A piercing howl echoes off the walls around us.

Bellamy groans. I glance at him and see his eyes squeezed closed. "No, not the labyrinth! He glances up the wall. Lord Oliver sits on a raised dais, looking down on us. Either side of him, beautiful

Narians attend him with fans, fruits, and fetish touches.

"Come Brother, do you not like to play games of strategy?" The howl of the beast sounds again, closer now. The Lord glances down the corridor and a smile curves his lips. "Better get moving. She's coming."

My heart races as I begin to understand the game he's playing with us. Instead of an invisible box, we have a chance to put walls between us.

"What's the point?" Bellamy snarls up to his brother. "You never let me win. I might as well let it end quickly."

Lord Oliver's face darkens, his brows come together in his fury. "You will play! Trust me, Jacob. While you are right, you will never be free of the games I play, I can offer you an incentive. The girl and boy can walk away forever if you all escape the beast."

I turn to Bellamy. "We can do this, Bellamy. There's a chance for all of us."

The familiar face of the captain looks down on me. His eyes are pale with a haunted hopelessness that makes me shiver. He gives a weary nod.

"I can't promise he will keep his word but, if either of you have a chance to make it out of this, I will do all I can to help you. Come on, this way."

I take Casper's hand and turn to follow Bellamy but Casper tugs on my arm, refusing to move.

"But," Casper whines, "I want to see the puppy!"

I turn to him. "Maybe we can play with her later, Casper. Right now we're going to try to solve the labyrinth. The exit is this way!"

I urge him to run with us instead of pulling away and we fall into step jogging behind Bellamy. He leads the way down the corridor and away from the growing growls and howls of the approaching chortessa.

We run what must be several furlongs before the corridor splits in a three way fork. A cackle of laughter sounds around us, echoing through the maze. "Eagrim's beak!" Bellamy swears. "It always changes."

Casper peers down each of the three paths. "Should we split up?"

My heart jumps. "No!" They both glance at me so I say more calmly. "We should stay together. The Lord said we only get out if we all get out together."

Bellamy nods. "Then which path?"

I bite my lip and gaze down each of the routes. Beside me, Casper falls silent and then points down the path to the right. "That way."

I turn to him. "Really? Why?"

"Because that's the way out."

I blink and gaze down the path he indicated. "How do you know?"

He shrugs. "The program says so."

A low growl behind us startles me and I spin to see down the long corridor. A pair of glowing eyes closes the distance between us.

"Any path is better than standing here," Bellamy says, charging down the lane Casper selected.

We continue weaving through the maze of corridors. At each intersecting point, Casper guides us through the next choice. The labyrinth continues in twists and turns. It seems unending. Behind us, Chortessa continues tracing us. She lingers, stalks, almost as if toying with us. We race forward, fleeing, rather than attempt to face her.

At yet another split in the path Bellamy stops in place and stares down each route. I pull up behind him. My breath is fast and gasping. My lungs ache. I lean my hands on my thighs as I pause to rest. Beside me, Casper seems to wilt. His face is pale and his little legs quiver with exhaustion. Even as tired as he must be he points down the path we should take.

Bellamy shakes his head. "It's hopeless, endless. There aren't any openings or anything, it just goes on and on."

Casper shakes his head. "You ain't lookin' right. It's full of openings, it's just you ain't seen 'em."

"What?" I ask, glancing around as if one might jump out at me. "Where are they?"

"There's one just across there, right in front of us." He points to one of the walls that separate the intersections. Each wall section is about three feet wide. They divide the maze into a series of corridors. I reach out and touch the wall Casper's pointing at but it's solid. It's dressed with intricate carvings that make a play of shapes in every direction but there doesn't seem to be anything unique or interesting about this particular section.

I shake my head and turn back to Casper. "But there isn't an opening."

"Course there is! It's written in the program. See?"

I turn back and watch the wall. "What? There's

just a wall! There's no way through."

The low growl of the Chortessa makes my stomach tremble and Bellamy glances behind us. A nervous tick jumps in his cheek. He swallows and glances at Casper. "If it's an opening, how do we go through?"

Casper blinks. "Oh! Well you have to open the door." He steps past us both and places his fingers on a marking. The panel of wall slides down into the floor and beyond it, a long dark corridor stretches into the distance.

Bellamy's mouth hangs open as he gazes at the chamber. "How–" He turns to me and Casper. "How is that there? I've never seen it before."

I shrug. "I guess things are not always what they seem in this place."

Casper grins. "Can't take anything for granted. It's Virreal, everything is a program."

I stand at the entrance to the long dark corridor. "Will this get us out of the labyrinth?" It looks like a darker version of the labyrinth. If it's the interior wall of the maze it might share it's endless twists and turns.

Casper seems to grow distant again. Before he responds a low growl sounds right behind him and the hulking form of the chortessa stalks toward us. I yank Casper forward, pulling him into the chamber. There doesn't seem to be any way to make the door close and with the chortessa so close, I can't see how we can outrun her.

"GO!" Bellamy shouts at us. Then he turns and faces the beast.

"But," I shout back, "we all have to escape or

none do."

"Casper's right, it's a program! You're not really here. I'm the only one who is. You just have to figure out how to wake up before she catches you. Go!" He steps toward the beast. She snarls at him. Her ears lay flat and she bares her teeth in a growl. "Chortessa's guts, girl! RUN!"

23

Plunged Into Darkness

Tye

I duck under the swing of another Stalker. His balance is terrible so, as he overthrows, I spin and kick him in the back of the knee. He stumbles forward, slamming his head against the wall as he trips. With a moment to catch my breath, I roll toward the door where I'd sent Niah. I can't risk them reaching her, but as I round up to face the remaining Stalkers, I reach down for the plasma pulser there. I complete the roll, coming onto the balls of my feet. I level the weapon at the nearest Stalker. I take another breath, exhale, and fire.

The plasma pulse creates a glow of white fire in the fading light. It lances toward a Stalker, plunging into the man's chest. He screams in pain as it scores straight through him. Then it slams into the head of the man behind him. They both crumple to the floor.

The third Stalker stumbles over their bodies. He lands face first in the dirt. "Chortessa's guts," he mutters, pushing himself back up.

I take the moment of distraction to dive across the alley and down a narrow groove between the buildings. The growing darkness helps to hide my movements. I duck out of sight and crouch low.

I'm hidden here. If I don't move, they won't hear me. Still, I aim the pulser back down the alley. If any Stalker comes looking for me here, I want to be able to take them out. I have room to move, but nowhere to go. The chill of the night is already descending and the fading light of the artificial suns leaves the streets in a haze of shadow.

Moments later, I hear a jumble of voices as more stalkers reach their fallen comrades. From my vantage, I can't see them, especially through the gloom, but I hear them pound on the walls of the alley. They slam the panels as they try to work out where Niah disappeared. Thankfully, they're too dim to figure out how to open the wall.

Eventually, one of the men sighs. "Baull-scat, we'll never get through like this. Can't see an eagrim's beak."

"Garett," says another, his voice commanding. "Go report to the Lord. Ask for a full contingent and a compliment of sierra stars to help with the search."

"Yes, sir!" A young voice responds. I hear the tap of his boots as he salutes and then races off down the street and toward the Palace. The remaining men chuckle.

"What a compy."

"Won't see him again."

"Last thing he'll ever do."

"Should we keep searching?"

"It's getting too dark," says the commanding voice again. "Besides, shift change was half a factor ago. Let's knock off, boys. Drinks at The Tipsy Dome?"

"Yes!" chorused the others.

"Drinks at The Dome!"

Their footsteps fade down the street. I sigh, letting out a breath I didn't realise I'd been holding. I push myself through the small opening and back out onto the street. I have to move mostly by touch because of the darkness but I find the wall again and press the marker. It slides open. I can barely see through the gloom into the greater darkness of the chamber beyond.

"Eagrim's beak," I mutter. Niah is gone. I shake my head, but plunge into the corridor anyway. I slam the door closed and begin weaving my way toward the Palace.

Wish

With Casper's hand in mine, we race down the long corridor. Tears stream down my face as behind us we hear the gruesome sounds of the chortessa and Bellamy. His screams of anguish and terror echo off the metal walls.

"No!" Casper shouts, yanking out of my grasp. He turns to race back toward Bellamy but I grab his arm.

"Casper, we have to run away or it will get us too."

"But she's not supposed to be mean. She's not a

bad puppy. She won't hurt us!"

I want to shake the kid but force myself to take a breath instead. I bend slightly so that his eyes are level with mine and look straight at him. "Listen to me, Casper. And listen to that noise. That's Bellamy trying to fight off the chortessa. It's attacking him, and it'll attack us too. We need to run away. We have to escape."

Casper gazes into my eyes for a long moment. His own eyes are full of tears. We listen as Bellamy's cries become a gurgle, and then there is nothing but the sound of rending flesh, breaking bone, and the snuffling of a beast feasting on a corpse.

"Puppy?" Casper whispers. His legs crumple underneath him. He kneels on the ground, his head in his hands.

I crouch down beside him and place my hand on his shoulder. "We have to go, Casper."

He nods but I can tell he is done in. "Can you run?"

He shakes his head.

I lean closer. "Put your arms around my neck. I'll carry you."

The boy reaches forward and wraps his arms around me. I lift him as I push myself back to my feet. Casper tucks his head against my shoulder. I hold him tight, but with his weight and my own body already exhausted I can't run very fast. Still, every step takes us away from the chortessa and, I hope, closer to freedom, so I keep running.

Eventually, the long corridor opens into a large room. I glance left and right, searching for an exit.

"Chortessa's guts!" I shout, turning in circles. I search the walls for any means of escape beyond the corridor from which we'd just come.

A low growl fills the room. A shiver runs across my skin as I glance into the darkness of the corridor. A pair of sharp, blood-stained fangs coupled with rows of jagged teeth gleams in the darkness. Above them, a set of eyes lock onto us. The hulking form of the furry beast fills the doorway as it stalks toward us.

I step backwards but I know there's nowhere to go. I wonder if it's possible to shield the boy in my arms, but as the animal moves closer, I feel a sinking hopelessness. "What did Bellamy say?" I ask Casper but the boy is so heavy in my arms I'm not sure he's still awake. "It's just a program." As I try to remember the rest I glance down at the boy in my arms. "That's it, we have to wake up. Casper, wake up. It's just a program. Wake up."

The boy looks up at me with tired eyes. "You too, Wish?" I nod although I have no idea how. "Okay then." Casper's gaze turns distant and he fades from my arms. I suck a breath into my lungs and then sob. I'm not sure if it's relief or loneliness I suddenly feel. But the weight in my arms is gone.

Now I'm alone to face the beast.

Wake up? No one told me how.

Niah

With the tablet to guide me, I move swiftly through the halls and corridors of this strange interior world. I keep moving steadily toward Wish. When

215

I reach a section of the Palace that seems to hold a door connecting this segment to the interior of the building I hook the tablet into a socket in the wall and hack the door open. It slides sideways, opening into an empty hallway. I peer up and then down. There is no one moving nearby so I step into the room.

I glance down at the tablet again to choose my direction and continue heading toward Wish. The route through the Palace is relatively straightforward. The building is built for function and beauty so it's arranged in sensible wings and floors.

As I step into a larger chamber I freeze, seeing a well-dressed man. I drop back behind a nearby cupboard and wait for him to pass before darting through the room, up the stairs, and down a long corridor. Each step takes me closer to Wish until I stand at the door to the room where her dot has remained at rest.

I pause to listen. Soft sobs cross through the door. My heart begins to race. "Wish?" I whisper, pushing the door open carefully.

The room is empty except for two bodies laid prone across strangely glowing chairs. The person closest to the door is torn to shreds. Dried blood pools all around his body. I swallow the wave of bile that rises in my throat and lift a hand to my nose to block out the smell as my gaze turns on the other body.

"Wish!" I gasp.

I race around to her. Wires run from her face and ears and are threaded across other parts of her body. She's drenched in sweat and her breath is heaving in her lungs. In her sleep, she's sobbing.

I reach a hand to touch her wrist but she doesn't stir. Beneath my fingers her pulse is racing. "Wish, wake up. You have to wake up."

When she doesn't stir I glance instead to the strange device she's hooked into. I place the tablet on top of the system and browse through the console. Tye said it's some kind of virtual reality. It may be dangerous to unplug her.

I look at the cords threading out of the machine and into my sister. A similar set still dangles from the remaining threads of flesh on the dead man beside her. I step to his side and grit my teeth as I pull the headpiece free of his skull then turn back to Wish.

"But if I go in after you, we both might be stuck," I whisper, looking down at Wish as I use the edges of my cloak to wipe clean the headset. I reach to pick up the tablet and use the adapter Lyris gave me to hook into the console.

The code is barbaric and convoluted, but it's built on the same basic structure as that used to program Elixr and Hart. It's a jumble with very little order or logic but I find it relatively easy to build in a subroutine that can wake us up in one factor. Surely that would be long enough for me to find Wish in that world and bring her home, here, to her body.

I activate the command then lay the tablet down. I climb into the chair with Wish. I gaze across at her one last time before sitting back. I fit the headset over my eyes, nose, and ears, then allow myself to enter the world the Lord created.

24

At Tooth and Claw

Wish

In the frame of the door, the chortessa snarls. A dollop of saliva drips from its gums and slips to the floor. I swallow, keeping my eyes fixed on the beast. Around me, the room begins to vibrate. At my feet, a layer of dust puffs up from the floor. Tiles on the walls rumble and clatter to the ground.

I glance around but the chortessa growls when I take my eyes from her so I look back. She fades behind an intricate shimmer of energy. I gasp as I recognise a face in the strange warping of reality.

"Bellamy?" Then the face crystallises and I realise it's not the captain. "Niah!"

Niah

I spent ages flicking through the various internal settings of Virreal's intricate programs until I finally found it. An echo of Wish led to this place. I glance around at the eerie shadows as the virtual world shimmered into existence around me.

"Wish!" I cry, seeing her standing there, awake and whole. My head dances and I grin, lifting a hand to wave. The joy on her face is fleeting. It's devoured almost instantly by panic. She gestures wildly behind me. "What?" I say, turning in place. I gasp as a large, furry, four-legged beast takes a step toward us from the narrow doorway.

I take several steps backward, then feel the solid wall behind us. Wish reaches out to grasp my hand. I grip hers in mine.

"I shouldn't have used a timer," I mutter. Wish glances at me and I shake my head not wanting to waste my breath explaining.

The chortessa stalks forward again. Beside me, Wish shivers and I can feel the terror dancing through her. I take a breath, trying to steady my thoughts. The beast fixes its gaze on my sister. I wave my free hand and take a step toward it.

Wish's hand tightens on mine and she tries to pull me back but I focus on the lesser beast. Its fixed look remains on Wish and it growls low in its throat. I narrow my gaze, studying the creature.

Curious. It seems obsessed with her, to the point that it's practically ignoring me. That reminds me of something Tye said when the eagrims attacked the guards.

"Wish, calm your mind. I think it's sensing your fear."

She shakes her head. "I can't not be afraid, Niah. That thing's a killer. It ripped the guard apart. And it," her voice sticks in her throat and she sobs again. Sniffing a breath through her nose she adds, "and

Bellamy."

I close my eyes because it doesn't make much sense, except I suppose it does. In a virtual reality, anything can exist and I can't be sure this particular creature isn't programmed to be a vicious killer.

Wish takes a deep breath. It shudders from her lungs but she dries her tears and lifts her chin. "But Casper, he said it was friendly." Her voice quivers with hope.

I glance across at her. "Casper?" She nods. I have no idea who she is talking about but since it seems to give her strength I let it go. We don't have time to run a blow-by-blow. "So," I say instead, "breathe. Calm your mind, Wish. Let's be her friend."

We watch as the chortessa's snarling softens in her confusion. She pauses, sniffs the air, and then puts her head low to the ground as she growls again.

Beside me, Wish quivers. "What if it doesn't work?" she whispers. The chortessa's lips curl, baring its sharp teeth. Its tail swishes in a slow drop and it takes another step closer, watching Wish with its sharp eyes.

"That's fear talking Wish. You have to really believe."

"We should run, Niah. Back down the corridor, back to the labyrinth." She lets go of my hand and begins to edge away around the wall of the room. The chortessa lunges forward then, snapping and snarling at her. Wish freezes in place.

I step between the beast and Wish. By breaking its eye contact with Wish, I force the creature to acknowledge me. "Hey!" I shout. "Leave her alone!"

The beast's low grumble echoes around the room. My confidence doesn't make it back down or show any signs of a friendly reception. I swallow as I see the way it sizes me up.

"You're right. We should run." I wave a hand beside me to indicate to Wish that she should continue to edge around the room toward the corridor. I match each step she makes, keeping myself between her and the chortessa. The beast's eyes follow me. It circles in place at the centre of the room and snaps it's drool-soaked jowls at us with low growls.

As we reach the corridor Wish grips my shoulder. "Let's run now, Niah? Please."

I nod. "On three." I flex my legs. "One." I keep my gaze fixed on the chortessa. "Two..." She's inching closer, her sharp claws dig into the hard ground. "Three." Wish darts away. I turn, sprinting after her through the long corridor, and hear the beast lunge after us into the darkness.

The passage continues like a long, dark series of channels. Wish darts here and there at intersections. I wonder if she knows the way or if terror makes the choices for her. Behind us, the chortessa snarls and yips. She's always close, but somehow, we manage to stay ahead of her. Barely.

The darkness seems almost endless. My heart is racing, my lungs are burning, and my calves are on fire as we run as fast as we can manage. It can't possibly be fast enough because the chortessa's long strides sound with soft pads against the floor behind us. Wish bursts through into the brighter light beyond the long corridor. I race to follow. I glance back over my shoulder at the chortessa chasing our heels.

Something heavy slams into my feet and I trip, stumbling over. I crash into the ground. The breath hisses from my lungs and pain ricochets through my hands and knees. I wince, trying to roll away but come face to face with the bloody, horrified features of my doppelgänger. His mouth is frozen open in terror, his eyes wide but dull with lifelessness. My heart stills and my breath catches.

Wish screams, startling me back to action. I roll onto my back as the beast lunges forward toward me. Its fangs seem huge.

I raise my hands to shove back the beast. They meet the wall of its heavy chest. Her weight is crushing. She's bigger than I realised. All I hear is Wish's screams and the heaving breath of the chortessa. The smell of its taints my nostrils. The sticky heat of its breath on my skin makes me want to retch.

My hands grasp in its fur. I try to throw it off me but I'm not strong enough. The beast's mouth, wet lolling tongue and sharp fangs, wraps around my throat. Then everything seems to shimmer around us.

My hands thrash and all I see is darkness but the weight is gone. In its place is an uncomfortable tightness over my eyes, nose, and ears. I lift my hands and wrench off the headset, throwing it across the room as my lungs heave for breath.

I turn to Wish. She's sitting up and tugging at the cord around her head. I help pull the headset off, let it drop behind her, then detach the rest of the wires connecting her to the machine.

"Niah! Niah!" She cries, reaching for me the moment our hands are free. She clasps me tight, sobbing hard against my shoulder.

Tears stream down my own face and I feel my breath tight in my lungs as I clutch her to me. I run my hand through her hair and just hold her tight and close. I don't want to ever let her go.

25

Old Friends Reunited

Tye

After navigating through the darkness of the Inner Circle's maintenance corridors, I finally reach the entrance to the Palace and begin making my way through the halls. I'm not too sure where to go but I see a large room open up in front of me. I glance around. There's no one in sight so I move to dart through, heading for the stairs. When voices break the silence, I freeze in place.

"If any of them escape, I'll have all of your heads!" A tall man strides into the room. Lord Oliver. My breath catches in my throat. I try to slink back, fading into the furniture. The Lord snarls, "Bring them to me, now!"

Several Stalkers walk into the room behind him. Their dark eyes scan the room briefly as if they're habitually used to assessing for danger. A commander turns to his men and gives a command with a silent flick of his wrist.

I duck out of sight as the three guards turn

toward me. They rush past me and down the corridor. I glance back at Lord Oliver before darting through the doorway to follow them. I move swiftly and silently through the hall, tracing their steps. They make their way through the corridor and then upstairs before coming to a door that stands ajar.

The guards pull their weapons and put their backs up against the wall as they ready themselves to breech the room. I raise my plasma pulser, firing three successive shots. They slam into their victims, hard and true, searing through flesh and bone to leave scorch marks on the walls behind them. The Stalkers' bodies fall in awkward angles. Their absent eyes gaze at nothing as I streak past them into the room.

I grimace, steering clear of the entrails and blood trailing out of the Virreal unit nearest the door. Crouched behind another unit, I see Niah and her sister. Their faces are pained and tear stained. The girl, Wish, looks like she's been through the wringer. "You two okay?"

Niah nods. "It was a close call, but we got out."

"What happened?"

Niah recounts what she knows and Wish fills in what she can. When they talk about the chortessa I feel a spark of hope. "Lord Oliver has a chortessa? A captive pet?"

Niah turns to Wish. "Do you think it was real?"

Wish nods. "I don't know. I don't know if anything was real in that place." She turns to her sister. "But you were there. You were really there, weren't you?"

Niah nods then turns back to me. "Does that mean there may be a chortessa strapped into a machine somewhere?"

I nod, excited. "Yeah! It's Ally, it has to be!"

"Ally?" Wish asks and I realise they don't know. Most of the Faithful remember the chortessa pup that was my constant companion when I was little. We had been inseparable. "I raised her as a pup when her mother got killed in a Stalker trap." I tell them. "The Stalkers captured her about a narcycle ago. Casper was certain she was still alive. He'd tell me all about Lord Oliver's puppy. Where do you think she is?"

Niah's eyes seem to shimmer with a sparkle of her thoughts. She lifts the tablet from the top of the console. "Let's find out."

She plugs the device in and taps at the screen. I glance at the door and wonder how long it will be before another regiment of Stalkers is sent to find out what happened to the first. "How long will this take?"

Wish smiles at me. She seems more subdued than my memories of her on the mini-zip and the mamot, but her smile shows a warm allegiance as if she is sharing an inner secret. "It won't take long. Niah's real good with tech and programs. But she gets a bit lost in them, give her a decca." I nod and move across to the door to keep an eye down the hall. The bodies still lay unmoved and the corridor is empty.

"There!" Niah says, stabbing a finger at the tablet. She unhooks the device and turns toward me. "Let's go," she says. Wish falls into step behind her and they cross to me at the door.

I glance out again. "Which way?"

Niah points to the left and we move carefully into the hallway. We tread, silent but quick, down the corridor. I want to lead but I don't know the way so I let Niah step in front of me. She refers to the screen at intervals but moves steadily with a sureness of foot.

As we come on a larger room, there are voices ahead of us. I tug Niah back and we duck into a groove between some furniture just before a small party of Stalkers rushes past us. Niah sighs beside me. "Thanks," she whispers before pausing a moment to listen for more danger. Once the Stalkers pass, we duck out of our hiding place and move swiftly across the room to the north.

We continue to weave, heading down stairs and along passageways until, eventually, the walls around us turn earthen and dank. I bite my lip, realising we must be getting close to where they've been keeping Ally. It doesn't look like her quarters will be any lap of luxury.

"Nearly there," Niah says quietly. I nod. We round another corridor. "There's a second life sign here. It paces up and down the long corridor at regular intervals so I think it might be a guard."

"Step back and let me go ahead." I tap the side of the pulse weapon with one finger and then hold it in front of me as I step to the corner of the intersection and peer around. The guard is walking toward us. He spots me and cries out but I fire the plasma pulser. The lance of energy cuts through him, silencing his cry.

"Someone might have heard that!" Wish whispers.

Niah glances at the device. "Yeah, there's movement to the north. We have to be fast. There is about a furlong between us, several doors, but if we're not quick they'll be upon us in deccas."

We dart down the hall and Niah pulls us up in front of a dark room with heavy iron bars. It looks like one of the ancient prison cells from the old histories of Nar. A sopping mountain of mangy fur is sprawled across the cold floor. It jerks from time to time like a pup that's dreaming. I slam against the iron door but it's locked.

"Step back," I call as I do exactly that. I aim the plasma pulser at the door and fire. The lock and frame buckle as the metal melts away. I shove the frame of the door again and it swings inward. "Stay here. It's been a long time, she might not remember. She doesn't know you. She'll be frightened."

"Won't she need to be untethered from the program?" I glance back at Niah, who holds her tablet. She fumbles for the right adaptor to plug into the old system built directly into the wall of Ally's cell. "I'll do this, you go to her. I'll try to wake her up immediately."

She hooks in as I cross to kneel beside my chortessa friend. She is torn and battered, bruised and bloodied. Her teeth are rotted and the cords of the Virreal device jut out of her as if they grew out of her fur. In ticks she stirs, whimpering.

"Okay, you can unhook her now. She's awake."

"Ally girl, shhh." I keep my voice calm and

smooth, trying to help her remember the way we always talked together. "It's me, Ally girl. It's Tye. I've come for you."

She whimpers so pitifully that my heart aches, but her tail lifts in a half-hearted attempt to wag. I detach each of the cords from her and tug them out of her matted fur. The process feels like it takes an age but can't have taken more than a few moments.

"Two furlongs," Niah whispers from across the room. She's already unhooked the tablet and is waiting with Wish beside the door.

"Come on, Ally. We've got to go." Ally looks up at me. Her eyes are wild and pained but I see the hint of recognition there. She tries to get to her feet, stumbles, and falls back in a heap. She gazes up at me. I can tell she's not sure she can trust me. "Hey girl, it's okay. We'll get you out of here."

I tug the large beast into my arms. She's heavy but so malnourished and withered that I can heft her in my arms without being crushed.

I glance at Niah. "Can you guide us out of here? We have to go."

She nods, and we streak back down the hall. We weave carefully through the maze of the Palace's rooms and corridors until we can disappear into the narrow passages between the Palace and the city. Eventually, we make our way through the shadows. With each step, we head back to the chapel.

Niah

The way Tye cradles the chortessa in his arms

makes my heart ache for them both. She must have once been a truly beautiful animal. Now she hangs in tattered ruin across Tye's strong arms. Her head lolls against his shoulder each time his steps jostle them.

We weave our way through the strange shadowy interior walls between sections of the city. The long corridors twist in patterns around the borders and create a passage that allows us to completely bypass the streets of the Inner Circle.

As we cross into the Outer Circle, the corridors are less numerous. From time to time, we dart out from them in one place and enter them from another. I'm thankful for the lightless streets of the Outer Circle. It makes it hard to see where we're going but it also means we won't be observed by others. Despite looking a lot like a ragged blanket of fur, Ally would definitely draw attention.

Eventually, we reach the chapel. It's lit from within by a soft glow of candles. Tannan, Jenin, and Blake are pacing the large hall of worship when Wish and I push the doors wide for Tye. He carries the chortessa inside.

"Where have you been? The alert went up factors ago. We thought you'd been taken!" Jenin says, rushing forward.

Blake grins behind her. "We were making odds on who was most likely to need to be rescued."

Tannan pushes them both aside to come forward. He glances at the blood-soaked beast in Tye's arms and waves us toward the chamber that leads down into the catacombs. "We better get her looked to. No time to waste. Jenin, Blake, secure things behind us, will you? And blow out the light. We don't want the Stalkers to have reason to look for them here."

They nod and the rest of us move into the catacombs. Tye shifts Ally to one shoulder but it still takes time to navigate the ladder. Tannan helps him down but I can see by the way the muscles in his upper arms quiver that he must be exhausted.

He turns to me when we reach the ground. "I need to get her seen to, will you be okay on your own?"

Wish steps up beside me and wraps her fingers around mine. "She's not alone. I'm not leaving her. You can't make me!"

Tye's wry smile makes me smile, too. "He didn't mean that silly," I say to Wish. The smile I give Tye is shy and I nod. "We'll be okay. I want to check in on Hart."

"Right, the bolt trap. Do you remember the way?"

I nod, not because I do remember but because Tye looks like he's about ready to drop. Besides, I already checked the tablet so I know the maps extend down here. What's more, there seems to be what looks like a homing beacon set to guide the way back to the droid's main unit. Hart had clearly been a phenomenal work of technology to be able to build dynamic maps from the supersonic sonar pulses this little tablet must produce.

Tye's gaze lingers on me a moment and we both stand in silence until Wish shifts on her feet beside me. Tye breaks the gaze first, glancing at her. Then he nods. "I'll find you as soon as I can." He moves off down the corridor and I lead Wish to the tech lab.

As we enter the lab, Wish lets go of my hand and immediately begins exploring the shelves and tables. Oblivious to Lyris, she rummages through the gadgets and parts, assembling parts as if it's all second nature to her.

"Niah! Wish! You returned for me!"

I smile as I hear Hart's familiar voice. "Hart!"

Wish turns to him and shakes her head. "Not my idea, rust bot. Your circuits still scrambled? Screws still loose?"

Hart's blue orbs blink as they'd always done. His head tilts as he considers her. "Actually, I am much restored–"

"Yes," Lyris says, interrupting him. "In fact, we've been having quite a conversation. About clones, and missions, and cures."

I feel an uneasy pit rise in my stomach.

"Blake and Jenin brought this back from the edge of the Outer Rim." She lays a tall black cylinder in front of me. I release the breath in my lungs as I realise what it is.

"Is that the fabrication drive storage from the drill platform?" Wish asks, crossing the room to us.

"Hart seemed to believe so. I got the impression it was important that you have it. Something to do with an ore you need?"

I nod. "What else has he been telling you?"

"He tells me you really are Bellamy," she pauses, as if giving me a chance to refute it, but in my heart I know there must be a degree of truth in her words. I'd seen him myself. His real face, even frozen in horror and death, was too much my own.

Lyris continues, "In fact, he tells me that you're here to save the world."

I shake my head. "I'm not Bellamy. I can't be him and I can't bring him back." I pause, looking up to see Lyris's eyes on me. There's a dark yearning within them, as if even she has been waiting her whole life for a saviour. I swallow the uncomfortable lump in my throat, then continue, "I'll do what I can. I understand the technology but I have no idea if we can get it to work or even what it does if we can."

Wish glares at Lyris. "We didn't sign up for any of this you know. It's not fair to ask her to save your world. We don't even know you. We don't have to help you."

I turn and place a hand on Wish's arm. "But they helped us, Wish. They didn't have to but they did. And we're going to do what we can, too. We might not have been created on this world, but it was Bellamy's home and, somehow, that makes it mine."

26

In The Shadow Of Stalkers

Wish

Starship, mini-zip, even mamot, I've travelled in style in the past but there is just something epic about striding through the furlongs cradled on the shoulders of a giant tiolf. The air, even murk-filled as it is, blows through my hair.

I crumple the tiolf's fur in my hands and lean low as Selnar leaps over a rocky outcropping. We sail smoothly and she lands on confident paws. Her claws dig into the dry dirt with every stride. My heart races as I feel the way her muscles move beneath me. We're united. I hadn't even felt this close to the mini-zip when I'd had the power of that tech beneath me.

I hear Niah's laughter and glance to where she rides on the tiolf beside me. She's wearing Bellamy's coat again. I'm glad to be free of it because I didn't much like being taken for him. I wonder if she hates it as much as I do.

Tye commands Ke-am and Niah sits behind him

watching me. She sits so close against Tye's back, with her arms wrapped around his waist and her head tucked between his shoulder blades, that it looks like she's hugging him. It reminds me of the satchel that bounces against my back and the fabrication drive within.

"What?" I shout, hoping my voice carries to her ears before it's whipped away by the wind.

Niah lifts her head from Tye's back and shakes it. "I don't think I've ever seen you so happy."

I grin. "This is wild. I don't know that I'll find riding a mini-zip exciting ever again."

We make swift progress over the dark space between the edge of the catacombs, the Outer Rim, and the small crater where Elixr kinda landed. Beneath me, I feel Selnar's tension as she approaches. She senses the unrest well before we can see it through the gloom and darkness of the Shadowland.

The tiolf band closer together. I'm almost brushing shoulders with Niah as we gaze out over a ridge to the ship below. Tye grimaces. "Stalkers."

"What are they doing here?" Niah's voice is tight and I can tell she's tired. I reach a hand out to hers. She squeezes mine as if she's reassuring me, not the other way around.

Tye strokes a hand down Ke-am's neck. "Lord Oliver must have sent out recon when he learned of you. The Elixr will be strictly off limits. He can't risk word getting back that Captain Bellamy has returned."

Beside us, Hart clomps to the ground. I glance at him, not sure if he fall off Farlem or chose to dismount the beast. His hover jets thrust to shove him upright and he glances around. "Well, really. Confounded rug," he says. He brushes his metal hands down the chrome panel of his chest as if dusting himself off. The blue orbs of his eyes narrow at the tiolf. Farlem leans over and runs a wet tongue across Hart's face screen. The droid's eyes go wide and he raises his hands to ward off the animal.

Tye ignores the robot and young tiolf. "We'll need to approach carefully."

Niah nods. They gaze at each other a long moment so I give up waiting for them and climb off Selnar's back. "Sneak tactics, right?"

Tye helps Niah down from Ke-am. She lands heavily on the ground. I notice her sway a little. She places her hand on the tiolf's hide to hold herself upright, steadying herself before Tye slides down to the ground too.

"You okay, Niah?" I ask.

She shakes her head. "I'm fine." She turns away, to gaze at the ship in the distance. "We should go. We don't want Lord Oliver to have an opportunity to destroy the cure."

I bite my lip because I can't help feeling like she's lying but there's nothing else I can do so I follow her and Tye to the edge of the crater. We climb over the edge, into the crater, and make our way through the outcroppings toward the ship.

Several Stalkers pace the edges of the light cast by Elixr. They keep a rough formation that is probably intended to keep people at bay. "Sneak past?" I suggest.

"And then what?"

I shrug. "Then we go release the cure."

I can see Niah thinking and eventually she nods her head. "Okay, but carefully."

Tye waves a hand signal to Ke-am and Selnar. They both crouch low along the edge of the crater. Beside them, Farlem copies their movements. He's more wiggly as he crawls across the ground, nudging farther and farther forward. The two older tiolf tuck their heads against their forelegs and keep their gazes fixed on the four of us as we make our way down the rim and toward the ship.

The Stalkers move in short circuits around the ship. Their formation is staggered rather than uniform. There are gaps in it that may make it easier to sneak past. As two stalkers turn toward the back of the ship, the two at the front turn toward us. I freeze in place because our position puts us directly in their line of sight. Beside me, Hart continues on, oblivious to the danger, but Tye and Niah dart behind a rise in the earth. Tye pulls Niah down beside him and they collide in the dirt. I glance around, wondering where I can hide.

As if sensing my danger, Farlem bounds down from the crater rim. The guards see his warm tanned fur as he strides toward us. Beside me, Niah calls softly, "Make a run for the ship, Wish. They haven't seen you."

I glance back at the guards who are aiming their plasma pulsers at Farlem. My heart stops as a streak of white fire lances forward. The tiolf darts aside with a yelp. He tucks his tail between his legs but keeps bounding forward.

"No Farlem! Go back!" I shout, racing back for the lesser beast. The Stalkers strike out toward us. Farlem dives into my arms. He's so big that his weight throws me down on the ground. I try to push him aside as he tucks his whole body close to me. He licks at my face and hands in a frenzy. "No you crazy fursack, they're coming! We have to run!"

A blast of plasma pulses past us. Between Farlem's panting breaths, I catch a glimpse of Tye standing to fire at the Stalkers. They return his shots. Beside him, Niah gets to her feet. She rushes toward me but freezes in place when a blaze of plasma cuts just inches in front of her and creates a scorching pothole in the earth.

It feels like Stalkers are coming upon us from every direction now. One grabs Niah's arm. She yanks back, pulling them both off balance. She recovers fastest and shoves the Stalker away. She tries to sprint toward me but the Stalker trips her. She lands with a hard thwack against the dirt.

"Niah!" I cry. Farlem startles at my voice. He raises his head, looking around at the frenzy of men. His eyes settle on Niah, motionless on the ground. He darts toward her but I tug him back. "No, Farlem! Go home!" The tiolf whimpers. He's stronger than me so he pulls out of my arms. He dashes toward Niah. A pulse of plasma streaks toward him but slams into the dirt at his feet. He yelps and darts away, this time racing toward Tye who is ducking another lance of hot plasma. He slams his own weapon against his open palm as if trying to get it working again, then tosses it away.

"Run!" he cries. He kicks away a plasma pulser from the Stalker nearest him and then raises his fists, slamming one into the chin of another Stalker.

The Stalker who knocked Niah to the ground grabs her arm and pulls her to her feet. She sways in place but still tries to take a swing at him. He locks his arms around her. She can't move.

I swallow, roll to my belly and push myself up from the ground. I race toward my sister, shoving the Stalker away from her. He swings at me. I duck under his clumsy arm, dancing away.

"Go, Niah! Run!"

"Wish!" she cries. The Stalker reaches to tackle me and I dart out from under him. Niah grabs his arm to hold him back. They tussle but I can see her growing weaker and weaker.

"Please, Niah! You have to get away!" Niah's breath is racing so fast. I can see the colour flaring in her cheeks. It reminds me of the way she looked in the infirmary before we could take her blood. "Please, Niah!" I cry, wishing she would stop because every moment must be making her sicker and sicker.

"You have to get away, Wish. Please!"

"I'm not going without you!"

"Chortessa's guts!" Tye mutters, slamming himself into another Stalker as he tries to reach Niah.

Two more Stalkers come upon us then. They hold me back. My arm aches as one of the two Stalkers grips it and pulls it up high behind my back. The other clamps his meaty fingers around my other elbow. I struggle against them, but their grip is so hard that every time I move it hurts.

Niah rushes them. She slams against the back of the one holding my elbow. We all stumble forward and I drop to the ground. As I push myself back to my feet, I reach and grab Niah's hand. I pull her with me as I try to run away. The Stalker nearest me grips my hair. I wince as he tugs, yanking my head back.

Tye jumps onto the Stalker's back. He stumbles, letting go of me, and I fall forward from the sudden lack of resistance. The Stalker rolls Tye off his back and throws him over his shoulder. Tye lands with a gasp. Niah tries to help Tye up but another Stalker grabs her arm. She yanks away.

I see it in her face the tick before her eyes seem to lose the spark of her consciousness. Her breath is rasping so fast in her lungs that I can hear it.

A Stalker aims his weapon at Tye and I gasp as his finger tightens around the trigger. Niah acts faster than I can. She rushes at the man. I see the colour darkening her skin. She stumbles at the last moment and falls, crashing into the man. Their collision throws off his balance. The plasma pulser skitters across the dirt and Niah and the Stalker land heavy beside it. Her eyes are closed. She doesn't move.

"Niah!" I cry out but she doesn't even stir.

Tye reaches for the plasma pulser. He fires at the Stalker before the Narian can recover. Then he lifts Niah into his arms. "Come on, Wish! We have to go!"

He's already racing toward the rim of the crater. He whistles and Selnar and Ke-am dive over the ledge. Ke-am runs close to Tye. He grips the tiolf's fur. The animal bends low as if scooping Tye up, and with a tight grip around Niah, Tye scrambles onto the tiolf's back. They disappear over the rim of the crater in ticks.

A streak of plasma spears past me. It slams into the hip of Selnar as she bounds toward me. She crumples, slamming into the dirt. Her body lands hard, rolling head over tail before coming to a stop. I hear a snarl behind me and glance back to see Farlem take down the Stalker who must have fired the weapon. The beast rips the flesh from the man's throat. The Stalker screams until his gurgling breath fades.

I turn to run back toward Selnar and the rim of the crater behind her but several hands reach for me. I'm surrounded. I thrash against the Stalkers but they hold me so tight that I can't move.

"Let me go you baull-scat void scum!" They laugh and I glare at them. They drag me back toward the ship. There's no sign of Hart. I wonder if the droid managed to sneak onto the ship, if he's been captured, or if he escaped. I struggle again, trying to pull away from the meaty hands clamping my arms.

A heavy thud slams the back of my skull and my head spins. Every part of me feels heavy. I hang loose in their meaty grip. My feet trail behind me, and I cling to the edges of consciousness, as the Stalkers drag me into the ship.

27

For The Cure!

Niah

My head's pounding. It's the first thing I notice before I feel the muggy air that smells of dirt and murk. There's a soft murmur of voices nearby and the fuzzy sound of their speech slowly takes shape into words as my mind reconnects with the world around me.

"What is it, do you think?"

"I don't know. She's really hot again." I recognise Tye's voice. It's soft and deep with concern.

"It keeps happening, doesn't it?"

The pause of silence between them speaks volumes. I know I need to break it but I'm not sure my lips are working yet. When I open my eyes, I'm glad for the darkness of the earthen walls around us. And even more glad that they're lit with the flickering glow of firelight rather than the bright lights of the Elixr. Even then, my eyelids feel so heavy that I can't keep them open.

"I'm okay." My voice is a croaked whisper. I

cough, feeling the tightness of my chest. My heart still races. I feel it pounding in my temples. I try again. "I'm okay."

A cool hand brushes back the hair from my brow. I want to sink into it because the cold feels so good against the hot flush of my skin. "Niah?" Tye's voice is gentle. His breath warms my cheek so I know he must be really close. I try to open my eyes again. His face is murk-streaked. His eyes are dark with worry. "You okay?"

I nod but the pounding in my head stabs my eyes. I blink, trying to fight back against the pain. I draw a breath as I fight to remember what happened. Then I remember and push my whole body upright. "Wish?"

Tye grips my arm to hold me steady as I sway. "Hey, go slow."

I turn toward him. "What happened to Wish? Where is she?"

I can see from the shadows in his eyes that the news isn't good.

"They took her," Tye whispers.

I nod. I'd already guessed it but hearing it from him makes my heart feel heavy.

Blake steps forward. "They've increased the guard but the Elixr is still open. The Shadows haven't noticed them bringing the girl or the droid out."

"We have to go get them." I gaze at Tye, imploring him to help me, but I know there's no way the two of us will have any chance against what is probably a whole contingent of armed soldiers now. I glance around at the others and bite my lip. "It'll take an army, won't it?"

Tye glances up at Blake. Blake shakes his head. Tye stares him down. "She's the one, Blake. You know she is."

"It's too great a sacrifice."

"It's not just one girl. It's the cure. We've been waiting two hundred narcycles. Isn't any sacrifice worth this?"

"We're Shadows, Tye, not Faithful."

"Baull-scat! The Shadows have always been Faithful. We might live beyond the Outer Rim but these people, this world, their hope for a better future, it has always been ours, too."

Jenin puts a hand on Blake's arm. "You know he's right, Blake. The Faithful would not ask it of you, but you're one of us." She turns to me. "We might be able to help you, too."

Hope swells in me for a moment then fades. "Even with four of us there won't be enough, will there?"

Blake sighs. "If Bellamy needs an army then we have one."

I swallow, hearing the dead man's name. I can't help feeling like it's carved on my chest. I bite my lip and shake my head. "You know I'm not Bellamy."

Tye touches my arm so I turn to him. "Niah, we don't need Bellamy. We need you." I glance around at them. Jenin nods.

Blake's eyes seem dark with sorrow. I'm not sure if he feels sad for me or if he's doubtful that any of us will succeed in saving anyone, let alone a whole world. I notice a tick in his jaw. He swallows, then steps forward and kneels beside me. "Niah, we need you, too."

A shiver runs through me at his words. They sit heavy on me, holding the weight of expectation. As if sensing my tension Tye turns to me. He lifts a hand to turn my chin so that we're face to face.

"Niah," Tye says with a whisper. His voice grows stronger as he continues, "I know you never wanted to be our Bellamy, but we need you. The Shadows live beyond the Outer Rim for a reason. We're outcast. We don't usually come together." I nod, trying to understand. I think he must sense the uncertainty in my gaze. His lips curve in a soft smile that caresses my aching heart. "They'll rally for you, Niah. They'll rally for the one who brings the cure. They'll rally for Bellamy reborn."

I shake my head and with a wry laugh, I say, "Was I even born?"

His grin sparks a light within me and he shrugs. "No idea, but however you came into being, I'm glad you're here. You can do this. We can do it together."

I nod. Tye grips my hand in his and I feel his strength coursing through me. Tye really does believe in me. He believes with such unwavering certainty that it feels easier for me to believe it, too, than to shatter his faith.

My throat is still tight but I force steel into my voice as I smile, nod, and say, "Let's do this."

Niah

I was able to rest for a few factors while Blake

sends word to call the Shadows to meet.

Now, we stand on a high ridge looking down into a valley of dark dirt. Beneath us, of a horde of Shadows gather. They stand, murk-covered and raggedly-clothed, gazing up at us. I wonder if they can see my face through the gloom of the Shadowland.

As Blake steps to the edge of the ridge, he thrusts a small stone into the sky. It flares into brilliant white light, casting a glow over the heads of the gathered Shadows and, I presume, illuminating those of us standing above them.

"Shadows, I thank you for coming," Blake calls. His heavy voice echoes from the canyon below. "We've waited two hundred narcycles, but at last, the circuit has arrived. The Elixr has returned. We have a cure."

The cheer of a hundred voices roars up from the valley. The noise echoes and the ground beneath us trembles. I feel my stomach quiver. All of these people are waiting for a miracle I'm not sure I can deliver. Blake turns toward me.

I take a step forward so I'm standing at the edge of the cliff. Beneath me, the crowd seems to roar louder than ever before. I swallow, suddenly uncertain what to say.

Tye steps up beside me. I feel his shoulder brush mine. "You can do this, Niah," he whispers.

I draw a ragged breath and gaze down at the faces beneath me. I force myself to feel Tye's faith, to feel Wish's courage, even Hart's certainty in my destiny. I exhale one last shuddering breath, fill my lungs again, and raise my voice.

"People of Nar, I stand before you." Their voices roar out again and I hear in their chanting chorus Bellamy's name. Draped in the shadow of his coat, I must look like him. I shake my head, raise my hands, and continue, "I have travelled from the far reaches of space. I bring you the cure. For two hundred narcycles, you have been made outcast by Lord Oliver and his City of Light. Now, at this final factor, your salvation is held hostage. I come to you this circuit to plead your help. I cannot do this alone."

As one, the Shadows raise their hands in the air. I feel the energy of them pulsing toward me. They truly believe that there is a future beyond what they've experienced these two hundred narcycles. None of us know what the cure will deliver and yet every single one of them dreams of a circuit beyond it. These people will rally, and we will take down the tyrant.

Beside me, Tye calls out. "Lord Oliver has taken the Elixr. She, and the cure, are held captive. Together, we must retake the ship. His men are well-armed and numerous, but together we can triumph."

"Bellamy!" The sound of the dead man's name on the lips of these people makes me cringe. I raise my hands to quiet them.

"I do not wish to mislead you. I'm not Captain Jacob Bellamy!" I cry. A few angry shouts rise up from the crowd but others hush them to silence. "My name is Niah, designation November-One-Alpha-Four. I am a clone. I was created on the Elixr to complete Captain Bellamy's mission." The gasp of their shock slows my heart rate. I pause a moment, waiting for them to be ready for what I'm about to say. "He died a brave man, sparing his crew, saving all of Nar."

A combination of outrage, disbelief, and grief washes over the crowd. Their voices rise in uproar. I fear I've lost them. Beside me, Tye cries out. "Please Shadows, you must listen." The Shadows fall silent, clearly respectful of Tye's presence. Tye continues, "She may not be the captain returned, but she is the only hope we will ever have."

I place my hand on Tye's arm then turn back to the crowd. "I am not Captain Jacob Bellamy," I cry again, "but I will complete his mission. I know how to deliver the cure. Right this moment, Lord Oliver seeks to destroy it. We must retake the Elixr. People of Nar, will you stand with me?"

Blake steps forward. "Shadows!" He roars. "I stand behind Niah. I'm with her. Will you stand with us?"

Tye cries out, "I stand with Niah! For the cure!"

I smile, then turn my gaze down on the crowd. "For the cure!" I echo. I pump my fist in the air and hope they go with us on this.

My breath races as our cry is taken up. "For the cure!" they cry in unison, again and again.

"To the Elixr!" Blake shouts.

As one, the wave of Shadows marches on the ship.

28

Storming The Starship

Tye

My people stand behind me and as we crest the ridge, the Elixr comes into sight. The ship engine's are humming. I wonder what Lord Oliver intends and then I see it.

The ship's guns, equipped with high powered plasma rifles and ion cannons, swivel in place. They're manned and ready to defend. Surrounding the ship, his troops create a three-man deep barrier. Even with one hundred Shadows behind me, we are outgunned and outnumbered. My heart sinks, but I lift my chin and focus instead on what's possible. Loss, but not defeat.

"Oh no," Niah whispers beside me. "How will we ever get through that?"

I look at her. "We don't have to take them all down. We just have to get through to the ship."

Blake growls, "Chortessa's guts! We could punch through the men but those guns will take us out before we ever reach them."

"I have an idea." Niah reaches into a deep pocket in Bellamy's coat and pulls out Hart's tablet. "Why didn't I think of this before?"

"What is it?"

"Hart has a direct link with the Elixr. We can control the ship from here."

I lean over, trying to make sense of what's on the screen. "What do you mean? We can control their guns, their thrusters?"

"Well, we can't fire the cannons remotely, especially while they are manned. The Narian controls override us. But we can prevent them from firing at us."

"That, at least, takes out that problem. What about men?"

"Well, it's like you said, we just need to get through to the ship. If you can get me onto the ship, I can release the cure and find Wish."

"We can," I say.

Niah turns to me. Her smile is as radiant as both solars combined. I catch my breath, my heart racing. We can do this, we have to. I turn to Blake.

"Blake, can you get us through?"

Blake's face is lit up too. I can see his eagerness to get into the fight. "We'll hammer those men so hard they'll forget which way the solars rise in the City of Light."

Jenin touches my hand. "Be careful, Tye. Lord Oliver won't consider mercy when he finds you. You're expendable to him, but not to us."

"I'll be careful." I turn to Niah. "Let's go."

We make our way down over the ledge toward the ship. The guns swivel toward us but with a few commands Niah directs their aim into the sky.

"I can take care of the ship's guns," Niah says, "but what about theirs?" She points to the Stalkers. The men in the forward line turn their plasma pulsers against us.

From either side of us, a troop of our Shadows pulls into formation. They charge forward like a spear. My heart aches as I hear the blasts of plasma. Lances of laser fire hit their marks. I can't see our men fall, but I hear their cries. I can hear their sacrifice.

Beside me, Blake grips my elbow. "For the cure," he says quietly. "Go, Tye. Make their deaths count. You must complete Captain Bellamy's mission."

I nod and take Niah's hand in mine. She grips my fingers. I feel the heat burning through her skin. "You okay?"

"I can do this."

Through the channel of Shadows, we charge forward. Either side of us the battle rages. Shadows and Stalkers confront each other. Our Shadows are armed with an arsenal of scrap weapons foraged from the land but they face the superior fire power of the Stalkers' plasma pulsers with courage. Around us, men fall in agony, pierced or singed by the weapons.

I force myself to ignore their pleas for help. We race forward to the doors of the ship which are just feet away, but between us stands another row of men.

I glance at Niah beside me. She has to make it. As if sensing my decision, she turns to me. "No, Tye."

"You have to do this Niah. I can't do it for you." I

feel her fingers tighten around mine but I pull away.

"Don't leave me."

"I have to make sure you get inside."

With one last look, I lean forward and brush my lips across hers. I want to linger, but I force myself to break away. With a roar, I charge toward the Stalkers. They stand firm as I rush them. I ram my shoulder into the nearest Stalker. His chest is like a rock wall but his feet shift and he falls to the ground. I turn and kick another Stalker out of the way. For a moment, there is a break in the line. Niah has a clear path.

I glance at her as she hesitates. "Go, Niah! Now!"

I see the streaks of her tears as she runs past me. I try to follow, but slam into a Stalker that charges forward to stop her. His thick hand grips my arm and he pulls me backward. I sigh as Niah disappears into the ship. Then, I turn to face my challenger.

Niah

I glance back but Tye's face is lost in the sea of Stalkers. "Tye," I gasp. My voice is a whisper as his name breaks on my lips.

I swallow the crushing weight of my fear and suck a breath into my lungs. I force myself to turn away from the chaos of battle outside the ship and instead make my way through to the lift. My temples throb and I hear the pounding of my heart in my eardrums. Time is running out. I can feel it in the swirl of my stomach and the heat of my skin. If

I'm going to do this, I need to do it quickly, before my body betrays me again.

I stand in the lift as it travels up. I step out into the corridor and try to remember the way to the core. I don't think it was near these crew quarters, was it? I grimace, then I remember the tablet and pull it free from Bellamy's coat.

The display flickers as it takes a moment to gather feedback. A map appears, detailing the long corridors, the lift, the crew quarters, the med lab. Ticks later a small blue light starts to flash and the display flickers again, turning three-dimensional as it scatters multiple ship layers across the screen.

Homed in, the little blue flicker idles in a small room one floor down. "Hart?" I gaze at the beacon, and the small white dot pacing nearby. "Wish!"

I turn back to the lift and race inside. I gasp in relief as the doors open on the empty corridor below. I head into the port wing and past the rec room. The cells beyond seem to serve a double use as both brig and storage.

Wish glances up through the bars as I walk into the corridor. "Niah?"

"Wish!" I cry, throwing my arms around her through the bars.

She hugs me back, then pulls away, her lips turned down with concern. "You're hot again, Niah. You're sick, you need to rest."

I shake my head. "There's no time. The Shadows are fighting the Stalkers. They're buying us the time we need to release the cure, Wish. We have to complete the mission."

Wish shakes her head. "Lord Oliver's men took

the fabrication drive."

Hart's jets hum as he crosses the cell toward us. His blue orb eyes are sharp and sparking. A thin line of blue cuts across his face. Twin eyebrows dip in a furious glare. "They've disabled Elixr."

"What do you mean?" I pause to listen, then add, "Her engines are humming. Can't you hear them?"

He makes a low growl. "They disabled her automation and took control by force."

"Oh." I plug the tablet into the system controlling the cell door. It's a simple hack. With the Elixr's systems down, there's no defensive line and the whole unit acts without any of its normal sentient systems.

Hart paces the cell while he waits for the door to click open. The sparks of his jets flare with red highlights.

Wish shakes her head. She pulls on the door as it clicks open. The metal bars swing inward. "We'll get her back, Hart. But first, we have to help Niah."

Hart nods. "Fabrication drive." The line of his mouth curves down. "Without access to Elixr's mainframe or my internal sonic system my navigation facilities are compromised."

I glance at the tablet in my hand with a frown. "You need this?"

His blue orbs blink and he tilts his head. "Indeed. My sonic system." He flicks open his chest cavity and pulls out a connection to link the tablet up to his main unit.

"Hang on." I flip through the settings, trying to memorise the route to the cure chamber. "Okay, I think I've got it."

I plug the tablet back into Hart's console and click it into place. I go to flip through his settings but the screen starts scrolling faster than I can read. I blink, then snatch my hands back as Hart closes his chest and turns to jet out of the door. "Stalkers are holding the fabrication drive in the cargo bay."

Wish turns to me. She grasps my fingers. "We'll get the fabrication drive, Niah. You get to the cure."

I gaze at my sister as my heart thuds hard against the wall of my chest. I don't want to leave her, to risk losing her again. She pulls me tight against her chest and I can't help but admire her courage. I'm supposed to be the big sister. How did she get so brave?

"It's okay, Niah. We can do this." She takes my arm and we walk back toward the lift. She raises her head as we near the corner, then turns to me with a grin. "It's not a tiolf, but it'll do." She nudges her chin to a mini-zip tucked against a wall as if stacked for storage.

"You don't even know if that still works."

She flicks the controls and it revs to life. She nudges it into the lift, turning it back to the doors. "Have some faith, Niah. We've got this!"

I laugh, feeling my heart lift at the way her whole body seems to light up with joy at the adventure of it all. I shake my head. The doors close and the three of us descend.

My heart shudders as the doors open on the next floor and Hart and Wish step out. I reach out, grip Wish's shoulder and pull her into a tight hug. "Be careful, Wish." I whisper. She strokes the tear from my cheek.

City Of Light

"You too."

29

This Way Or That

Wish

I watch as Niah disappears behind the doors of the lift. I don't want to leave her, but she needs me to do my part. With Hart, I mount the mini-zip and rev its engines. I hold tight as the craft moves beneath us. Carefully, I guide it through the turns in the ship, headed for the cargo hold.

Lord Oliver's men look up as I crest through the entrance to the cargo hold. One lifts the fabrication drive as if he's about to launch it through the air.

"No!" I shout and he freezes. I race the mini-zip directly at him. He cries out, ducking to the ground. He clutches the drive to his chest.

I whip the tail of the mini-zip to one side and kick my foot into the Stalker's gut. Air bursts from his lungs. His back slams against a cargo crate. The fabrication drive falls from his hands. It clangs against the metal floor and rolls several feet across the hanger.

I turn the mini-zip. It's rear end slips out behind

me a little, touching the edge of the crate, before I can right it. The Stalker ducks beneath and the hot fumes of the hover jets singe across his flesh. He raises his hands to his face, screaming as his skin sizzles. I push away, skimming the ground of the hanger as I race after the drive. It's cylindrical shape continues to roll across the floor. I zip past it and slam my foot to the ground to whip the mini-zip around again. The drive rolls to a stop against my foot.

Several Stalkers race toward me. I reach down and snatch up the drive, then pass it to Hart. "Niah needs you, Hart! As soon as you have the chance, you have to go. Don't look back."

I drive the mini-zip forward again. The jet engines blast over the top of the Stalker nearest. He cries out. His screams are piercing, pained. I grimace, but force back the gut-wrenching guilt I feel.

I whip the mini-zip around, spinning a series of tight circles in the hanger as I try to ward off the other men. The Stalkers scatter behind crates as the thrusters of the mini-zip blast searing heat toward them. I swivel again, turning the mini-zip toward the door of the lift. As we reach it, I arc to the side again, bringing the seat up beside the door. I slam my hand against the control. The doors slide open.

I pause to let Hart dismount. He launches through the doors. His hover jets thrust and he darts forward. He pushes a control inside the doors. The door closes between us. I breathe a relieved sigh and turn back to the cowering Stalkers.

As they rise from their crouched position behind the cargo crates, their gazes are fixed on me. I swallow, feeling their attention. But that's a good thing. I nudge the mini-zip, facing it to the large open door at the opposite end of the hanger bay. I focus on the darkness outside. I jet the engines, zipping forward, and zoom past the crates. I hear the men cry out as they give chase behind me. I duck as a lance of plasma sears by just inches from my head.

Outside, a host of Shadow people are overwhelmed by Stalkers. I bite my lip, wondering how any of us can have a hope of surviving this. A cry to the right draws my attention. Tye! He's fighting hand-to-hand. A Stalker's arm crushes around his throat and his cry is cut off as he gags for breath.

I steer the mini-zip toward him. I use the heavy metal rear to slam into a Stalker. I kick out at another. Tye hauls the Stalker over his shoulder. He slams the Narian into the ground then stands, hands on knees, panting.

"Thanks," he calls between breaths. "Niah?"

"She's okay, she's gone to release the cure."

He nods and turns to punch another Stalker. The man collapses to the ground. His plasma pulser slides across the dirt. Tye rolls toward it and picks it up, firing at another man racing toward us. Several more keep coming behind me.

"We're outnumbered, aren't we?" He nods, but doesn't look at me as he fires into the horde of men.

A blast of plasma slams into the rear thruster of my mini-zip. It starts smoking. I turn the craft to the lip of the crater and use its momentum to drive at the rim as the smoke gathers behind me. I'm pretty sure it must be hot enough to crack the heads so, before the motor dies, I rev the engines, twist the steering column, and turn it into the pit of Stalkers near Tye. As the mini-zip takes air, I lift up with my knees and dive backward of the craft. I roll down over the dirt as I put distance between myself and the spluttering machine. "Watch out!" I cry. Tye glances over, then darts away from the Stalkers trying to grab him. He dives into a ditch just as the engine explodes.

The blast throws me backward. I feel the breath slam out of my lungs as I hit the ground hard, but I've gotten far enough away that the flaming hot fuel doesn't reach me. Several Stalkers scream in agony as their skin and clothes sear from the blast. They collapse, dead or dying. I grimace and turn away. More men are coming.

I glance around, hoping to find a weapon or something to defend myself with. If we can just hold off until Niah releases the cure... We might not be able to save ourselves, or even Niah, but if she releases the cure then we save the rest of Nar and surely that's something. It'll have to be enough.

Six Stalkers surround me. I try to find Tye but either he's gone or he's dealing with his own problems. I swing at the nearest Stalker. He ducks beneath my arm then comes up behind me, gripping me tight. "Let me go, baull-scat!"

"Gosh, you're spicy for a little moon-skitter."

"Chortessa's guts, void scum."

His laughs softly and I shiver, stomach uneasy. I

try to pull away but his grip tightens, bruising my arms. I try to spin away, to sweep or stamp on his feet, but he holds me fast. "Easy there, little tiolf."

A low growl in the distance catches our attention. We look up at the ledge of the crater. Farlem stands there, his head low, ears perked. He gazes right at us. I go to cry out but the Stalker grips my mouth with his hand. I try to bite him. His breath hisses down the back of my neck as he gasps, but he keeps his fingers clasped tight over my lips.

Farlem howls. I feel the sound of it course through me. A chorus of howls follows his. Along the ledge, a line of tiolf form. I see Ke-am and Selnar step up beside Farlem. Between them, ragged and thin, but growling with fierce dark eyes, is the chortessa. And behind and beside them all are a thousand well-armed men and women. The Faithful.

White fire zips up toward them. The beasts dodge the plasma fire with a snarl, then launch themselves over the ridge and into the crater. The Faithful follow, rushing forward like an army of avenging angels. They throw themselves into the flurry of Shadows and Stalkers. The tiolf tear flesh and clothes and throats. I can't tell how they know which is friend or foe but their focus on taking down the Stalkers is reassuring. I feel the battle turn around us and hope blooms within me.

Farlem races toward me. My heart races with him. The Stalkers hand falls from my mouth. "Farlem!" I cry. The tiolf's ears perk up as he continues to stride forward. I gasp as I hear the weapon discharge beside me. The lance of plasma slips out like a streak of white lightening. It slams into Farlem's flank.

The tiolf stumbles, thrown sideways. He yelps but pushes himself back to his feet and charges forward. He leaps, and lunges for the Stalker holding me. I feel the man's grip waver and take advantage of his shock to pull away. I throw myself against the ground as the tiolf dives over my head and tears into the Stalker.

The tiolf tosses aside a severed limb, then limps toward me. His fur is smeared in blood but I stroke his ears as he nuzzles against me.

"I'm okay, boy. Thank you." I glance back at the ship. "Come on, Niah. We got you this far, where's that cure?"

Niah

As the lift rises through the decks of the ship, I feel around for some way to control access to the secret room. On many floors, the doors either side of the lift will open. You can enter or exit from both. But as it reaches the final deck, only a single door opens.

Beyond those doors, the long corridor to the main lab is dark. In the distance, light from the lab consoles casts long shadows. My heart races as I glimpse a hint of movement.

I turn away, searching the other door. I trace the cold chrome walls but there are no secrets beyond the primary control. The console itself is relatively simple. A handful of buttons, a jack, and a small slit. I wonder if maybe it's accessed by ID card.

An echo of memory brushes my mind. The image of a round disk flashes through my thoughts as if I'd unlocked this lift a hundred times before.

"The card," I whisper. I remember slipping the disk into the sleeve of my suit after hacking Bellamy's safe. I rub at the spot where the small sliver presses very lightly against my wrist. Before I can slip it free, the lift pings and the doors to the corridor begin to close. I gasp, step out, and watch as the lights show the lift descending through levels.

As swiftly as the lift descends, it begins climbing again. I glance around, wondering where I can hide. The corridor is stark and empty. Only the distant lab has any sort of cover, but who knows how many of Lord Oliver's guards might be in there.

The lift passes the floor below and continues rising toward me. I shake my head. "No choice," I whisper, then dart toward the lab.

It feels eerie to creep through the dim and silent corridor. It's as if the ship is dead. I'm surprised how much I've come to depend on Elixr in the circuits since I awoke. I swallow as I step closer to the lab doors and glance inside.

I freeze a moment when I see a dark shadow. A tall, blonde Narian stands with his back to the door. He gazes up at the large console window. Text streams down it. Then a red light starts flashing. The Narian slams his fist against the main workstation. "Chortessa's guts, Jacob. You and your baull-scat codes!"

I swallow, glancing around for a place to hide. I dart beneath the workstation nearest the entry. Behind me, the light hum of a small hover jet weaves up the long hallway. I see the swirl of blue purple jet stream. Hart!

I want to cry out, to warn him, but any sound, any movement might alert the Narian to my presence. Instead, I bite my lip and wonder what to do next.

Hart glides into the room. He acts as if he's completely oblivious to the Narian as he crosses directly to the fabricator in the middle of the room. My breath catches as I watch him slip the fabrication drive into the console. It hums to life. The Narian turns at the sound.

I bite back a gasp as I see the Narian's face. It's the image of Wish. Older, harsher, and shadowed with recognition and pain. Flashes of recall dance through my thoughts as a heart-aching connection courses through me. This must be Lord Oliver, but the flashes of Bellamy's memories in my mind reveal a greater truth. This is Captain Bellamy's brother.

"You!" he snarls. I pull back, suddenly afraid he's seen me, but his gaze is firmly fixed on the droid.

Hart reaches a hand toward Oliver as if giving a customary Narian welcome. "I am Harttade, a Hybrid Autonomous Research, Telemetry, Teleportation, and Defence Engine."

"I know what you are. My brother and I made you. What are you doing here?"

"My primary function is to repair, restore, and maintain the Elixr to optimum levels for the completion of her mission."

The Narian grimaces. He walks forward then begins to circle Hart. "Oh, of course that's what my brother would have you do. The most advanced Sentient ever created and he makes you a slave to his ship."

Hart turns in place to watch the Narian. Behind him, the fabricator beeps. I glance at the small, green, ready command that blinks across its screen. Almost as if he's trying to distract the Narian, Hart makes a bleeping bluster of his own and jets forward then spins in place. I hope it really is a distraction and not another malfunction.

He splutters. "My role is complete. My role is complete. My role is complete. The dispersal drive is fully functional. Nar waits for the cure."

He glances past the Narian directly at me. One of the twin orb eyes closes in a wink. I gasp.

"What are you on about?"

Hart blinks, looking back to Lord Oliver. "Oh, my apologies. I appear to be experiencing a malfunction."

Oliver waves him off. "Two hundred narcycles in the void of space with my void-scum brother. Bound to have a few bolts loose." He turns back to the console.

I glance at the drive one last time, hoping I understood Hart's message. With Oliver's back turned to us both, he fixes me with his gaze again and nods. I nod back and dart out from under the workstation. I race for the corridor.

"Hey!" Oliver cries behind me. I hear a crash of metal on metal. Part of me wants to stop, to check on Hart, but I know he'd rather I complete our mission. I gasp and sprint harder. A streak of white blasts past me. It slams into the wall, singeing a dark streak of molten metal into the chrome.

I pant, feeling the flush of heat on my skin as my heart pounds in my ears. My legs shake and I feel the weakness of my illness in every inch of my skin. I reach for the disk at my wrist as I slam into the lift. I turn, press the chip into the slit, then gasp as Lord Oliver steps through the door. He levels the plasma pulser in his hand directly at my chest.

"You're not going anywhere, moon-skitter." He glares at me. I feel a cold shiver as his gaze seems to devour me. "You're almost the perfect image of him. Almost." His lips curve in a cold, dark, smile. I swallow.

"I'm not him."

He chuckles. "No, but you're still trying, aren't you? Still trying to save the world."

I lift my chin and glare at him. "At least what I'm doing means something."

His gaze narrows. "Means something? We waited narcycles! Nar crumbled around us. I died a half-dozen deaths waiting for you. Millions of Narians died waiting. You think it means something? Your cure is two hundred narcycles too late."

I swallow again and try to blink back my tears. A big part of me worries that he's right. I have no idea what Bellamy's cure is or if it will help. This could all be for nothing.

I push back the drag of hopelessness as I hear the doors behind me slide open. Lord Oliver's eyes narrow as I step backward. Around us, a soft blue-green glow blooms.

Oliver steps forward. "Still so eager to throw your life away, Captain Bellamy?" he drawls. I see the strange green light reflected on his pale skin. It bounces off the chrome walls and glass windows all around us.

I shake my head. "I'm not Bellamy."

"No, you're not. Whatever did happen to my brother?" I step back again. Oliver follows. With each step I take backward he steps toward me. "There's nowhere to go, little moon-skitter. Nowhere to hide."

My hip bumps into something cold and hard. I glance down at the console. Oliver snarls. A bloom of white plasma slams into the metal at my hip. I gasp as it splatters searing plasma against my coat. I glance up at Lord Oliver. His cold, ice gaze fixes on me.

"Now, now. You know I can't let you be a hero." He steps close and I shrink away, circling him to keep a clear distance between us.

I bite my lip as I realise Oliver has put himself between me and the console. I can see it now. A tall cylinder of glass reaches from floor to ceiling. Inside, whirls a pale blue ocean filled with swirling light. On the command console thick numerals count down. Beneath the numbers a short command, 'Awaiting Release'. I gasp.

Lord Oliver waves the plasma pulser at me. "No getting ideas, now. We can't have that. Not at all. I have plans for you, little moon-skitter."

I fix my gaze on him. "What are you going to do

to me?"

His lips curve in a smile. "There are some truly marvellous things in Virreal. I created it you know. To give Narians something worth living for. I saved us."

"Trapped in a dome? Lost in a world that isn't real? Living for every scrap of staples they can muster? You call that saved?"

"If we'd waited for my brother they would all be dead!"

I glance behind Oliver again. The counter keeps ticking down. Nine, eight... Just inches from him is the release, but the white-hot death of his plasma pulser lies between us.

I can feel Captain Bellamy's mission pulsing within me as if it's all I was ever created for. Images of Wish and Tye flicker through my mind. I bite my lip, realising that everything we've done is greater than me, or even them. I didn't get to live my own life. This was bigger than any of us. This was all of Nar and all the Narians that remained. This could save them. This could save them all.

I hear the ping of the elevator behind us. Lord Oliver's gaze narrows. I already know who stands behind me. I feel her as if she's an extension of myself.

"I wouldn't," Oliver says. His voice is menacingly quiet. He fixes the aim of the pulser directly at me.

"No!" Wish gasps behind me.

Four, Three... I dart forward, terrified we'll miss our chance. Lord Oliver's eyes widen as he sees me dive at him. A burst of white fire slams into me. I feel the lance of heat and gasp. Instinctively, I lift a hand to my shoulder and feel the singed flesh and slick of blood throb through my fingers. Unable to stop my momentum, I plough into Oliver. We both crash backward into the column of glass.

I shove him back against the release lever. He snarls, pulling away and grips the console, but it's too late. A harsh hiss sounds around me and a blinding light slices up through the glass. I stumble and collapse to my knees. My chest burns. I'm not sure if it's the fire of plasma or the ache of my lungs struggling to draw breath. I try to block out the pain as I gaze upward. Around me, everything feels like it's swirling.

Another pulse of plasma bursts over my shoulder. Lord Oliver screams, lifting his hands. His eyes go strangely glassy and wild.

His body falls forward. His weight is crushing. We both crumple to the floor. Around us, a swarm of Narians fills the room. Wish is at my side. She's saying something, but I can't hear the words. The pain is overwhelming, drowning out all my other senses. Everything else fades.

In the silent tick before I lose consciousness, I wonder at the cure. Would I have survived if there'd been one for me?

30

Twin Suns Rising

Tye

Light soars out from the centre of the ship. It's almost blinding as it sears upward and slams into the clouds of murk. It scatters across the sky.

Around me, Shadows, Stalkers, and Faithful freeze in place, looking up. An odd mist starts sprinkling over us.

Rain? I wonder. We've never experienced it, not in my lifetime, not even in the City of Light. But this mist feels almost nothing like the description in the records of thrashing winds, heavy droplets, flooding plains. Instead, it blankets the land in a soft dew. It streaks trails of murk down the faces of the Narians around me.

The roar of an engine draws my attention away from the sky. A zip glider zooms out from the bay of the ship. Within, I catch just the glimpse of a cowled face – a Shadow? His passenger is a face no Narian could forget, Lord Oliver. I level the plasma pulser in my hand at them but they zip away so fast that they're out of range by the time I pull the trigger. The blast of plasma slams harmlessly into the dirt of the crater as the zip glider crests the rim, heading for the city.

Beyond them, a sparkle of light shimmers brighter than anything I've ever known before. It stabs my eyes. I raise a hand to shield my gaze as I watch half with horror, half with wonder as, for the first time in two hundred narcycles, twin suns rise over the horizon.

I swallow, awed, and fall to my knees as I watch in wonder. "She did it," I whisper. I close my eyes and feel the heat of the solars on my face. Around me, Narians roar with joy. I glance around with a grin. Stalkers, Shadows, and Faithful all embrace each other. They stand united, one people of Nar, no longer divided by the walls of the city.

Blake's hand slaps against my back. "She did it," he cries, an echo of my own words.

I nod, then glance at the Elixr. "Yeah, but where is she?"

Tannan, Lyris, and Jenin stand beside me. "Let's go find out," Lyris says. We turn away from the sunrise and head for the ship.

Wish

"Why won't she wake up, Tye?"

I hate the way my voice breaks. I'm not some little kid who can't let go. When I saw her collapse beneath Oliver, I thought she was dead. I'd breathed a sigh of relief to feel her skin burning hot. My relief was short because too hot was a bad sign too, but at least she wasn't dead. The dark, betraying part of my mind adds a soft, "yet" to my thoughts. My heart aches.

"They said she'd be okay." I turn to Jenin. "You said she'd wake up. Why won't she wake up?" I glare at her and at Blake who leans on the wall behind her. I wonder if Jenin had lied just to make me feel better.

The soft lights of the med lab blink in muted tones. They still haven't brought Elixr back online but Jenin seems to know her way around the consoles. The diagnostic bay hums and soft tubes go into and out of Niah's body.

Jenin places her hand on my shoulder. "She will wake up, Wish. Have faith. Your sister is very sick. The shock of the plasma blast to her shoulder, the sear at her hip, even her series of bruises from the nine-voids she's been through these last few circuits are taking a toll. It's good that her body is resting; it's healing."

"But she'll get better, right?"

Jenin nods. She glances at a console beside her as the sound it makes changes slightly. Then she turns back to me with a smile. "She'll be just fine. Look." She steps up to Niah's side.

I feel Niah's fingers tighten around mine. My breath catches and I lean close. "Niah?"

Her eyelids flicker, then flutter open. She swallows and runs the tip of her tongue over her lips as if they're dry. Jenin reaches for a bottle of spirit water as Niah tries to sit up.

Tye steps close beside her. He rests a hand at her back. She turns her gaze on him. It lingers there. I fight back the hint of jealousy I feel at the way she looks at him.

Niah takes a sip of water, then turns back to me. She squeezes my hand again. "I'm okay, Wish." She glances around. "Where am– What happened?"

Tye smiles. "Hey, there," he says, gazing down on her. "You're in the medical lab of the Elixr. You're safe. You did it."

"And Oliver?" The doors to the med lab open as Niah speaks.

"Don't you worry about that," Lyris says, coming into the room.

Tannan follows behind her. Then, the soft hum of hover jets precedes Hart as he enters behind them both. I'm surprised by the dance of joy I feel at the sight of the droid.

"I say, perhaps we should have him jettisoned into deep space. I found his company most unpleasant." The twin blue orbs of Hart's eyes seem to dance, then blink.

Lyris turns and shakes her head. "The Faithful will see to him."

"If the Shadows don't get him first," Blake mutters.

Lyris ignores him. "You did something wonderful for all of Nar, Niah. It's a miracle." Her voice breaks and she glances up through the sheen of tears in her eyes.

Lyris and Tye both peer through the large windows of the med lab. They gaze out at the bright sunshine. It casts light over the rolling hills and valleys. The Shadowlands were no more. The landscape is still barren but somehow, in the light and the sheen of moisture, there is hope that life will bloom there again soon.

Niah

Somehow, the light breaking over the Shadowlands is even more beautiful than the artificial suns in the City of Light. Almost as beautiful as watching the pulse of solars in the darkness of space. Almost.

Lyris turns back to me. "You have no idea what this means to us, to all the people of Nar, Niah. I don't know how we can ever thank you."

"But what happened to Lord Oliver?"

Blake shakes his head. "One of his baull-scat loyalists got him out of here in a zip glider."

Tye grimaces. "I can't believe I let him escape."

I turn to him. "He just walked away?"

Wish shakes her head. "He didn't. It was crazy there for a bit. I shoved him off you. He was hurt bad. I mean he might not even live because the plasma got him right in the chest. But I turned my back to check if you were okay and one of the Shadows pulled him out of there."

"A Shadow?"

Tye shrugs. "I saw him too, but I don't know who it was."

"Why would a Shadow help Lord Oliver?"

Blake grimaces. "Trust me, we'll be asking exactly that when we catch up to them."

Lyris steps forward. She places a hand on my shoulder. "Don't you worry about any of this, Niah. Our people will find them. Lord Oliver has no power now. The Faithful are already rising in the City. There's nowhere he can go."

I nod, hoping what she says is true. I squash the lingering doubt in the pit of my stomach. Oliver's smart. He's resourceful. We shouldn't let our guard down. I swallow and close my eyes against the pounding in my head.

I feel Wish lean close. Her fingers tighten around mine. "You're okay, Niah. Right?"

I glance up at her and squeeze her hand. I hope the touch conveys strength but worry she can feel my weakness. "I'll be fine, Wish. Don't worry."

"But your sickness..." Wish trails off and I wonder what she'd been about to say.

"Maybe..." I glance at Lyris, certain she can see the hope in my gaze.

She shakes her head and scans the console beside her again. A deep frown mars her forehead, making her appear older. She turns back to me. "I'll be honest, Niah. Your condition won't improve. The damage to your DNA is extensive. There's nothing we can do for you here. Even Elixr's medical technology does not have the means to cure you."

I feel the tension in Tye's muscles as he stands behind me. "What can we do then?"

There's a long pause. I bite my lip and try not to let the wave of hopelessness I feel crush over me. Then Blake steps forward.

"Actually," he says. All four of our gazes turn to him and he clears his throat.

"What is it, Blake?" Tye asks.

"Well, it's just a rumour, but you know what

those are like. We've had two hundred narcycles to turn fact into fiction. All of our legends might have truth buried within them."

"Just say it would you?" I can hear the frustration in Tye's voice.

Lyris places a hand on Blake's arm. "Do you know something that might help Niah?"

"It's in the Starscapes."

"Really?" Lyris asks, there's a soft wonder in her voice. "You've read the Starscapes?" I wonder what they are.

"Well, before my family were banished, my parents guarded Lord Oliver's library. I was little, but I remember."

I lean forward. "What do you remember?"

"There's a distant planet, I don't remember what it's called, but Nar used to trade with them for medical supplies. They were a first stop for Captain Bellamy's mission but I guess they didn't have a cure for the planet. Still, the Starscape Records indicate that they had a fix for pretty much every other ailment known to Nar at the time. If there's anything that can heal your illness, it will be there."

Wish practically bounces with excitement. "If it was Captain Bellamy's first stop, then it'll be recorded in our logs here."

Hope blooms within me, then fades as I remember the state of the ship. "But Elixr, she's grounded."

Lyris smiles. "We can fix her. There's nothing in Nar I can put a wrench to that I can't fix."

Wish grabs my hand. "Me too!" she says, "You do the codes, Niah, but I've got the metal. We can do

277

this! We have to!"

I swallow, smile, and nod.

As the others seem eager to get started right away, I turn to face the sunshine streaming in through the windows. In the warm light from solars that seem to dance around each other in the sky, I let myself hope.

Tye tucks himself close beside me. I feel the soft brush of his breath on the top of my head. I glance up at him as he gazes down on me.

"We'll find a way to save you, Niah," he whispers. "I'll do whatever it takes."

For now, at least, I let myself believe it's possible. But deep in my chest, where breathlessness drags on my lungs and I feel the pull of a sleep that might grip me forever, I worry that even if a cure exists, we might be too late.

Author's Note

Dear Reader,

I had an absolute blast writing this story. It's a deviation from my Blood of the Nagaran series and it's the truest science fiction I've written to date but I really loved getting into the technology and exploring space travel and programming. The thing is, this book was never intended. I was supposed to work on book four in the Blood of the Nagaran series for National Novel Writing Month in 2017 but when this story was pitched to me, I loved it so much that I couldn't resist. The concept was wonderful and I knew I could create a version of the story that would sing in my heart. I truly believe I've done that.

The fascinating thing about this opportunity is that it came to me in mid-October from the Smarter Artist writing community. Christine Royse Niles pitched the idea of having several authors writing to the same beats (story outline) in the 30 days of November with each of us ultimately ending up with our own unique version of the story. As a small group, we've followed each other's journey through the writing, shared our trials and triumphs, pushed and encouraged each other to succeed. And with every new scene I was fascinated to see how other authors took their stories in vastly different directions. Some versions of the Shadows of Nar are fantasy, others middle grade. Some have romance others don't. Some have young characters others are more mature. Each author brought his or her own style and voice and passions into that original outline and so each version of the story is unique and special.

For me, space travel has been something that's fascinated me for decades. I've always been a fan of Stargate, Star Wars, Star Trek, even Doctor Who. More recently I've loved the book (and movie) of The Martian, and Gravity, and in my youth, it was Alien. Space sciences have always been intriguing so it was a true delight to be able to delve into it.

Coupling that with my pre-author life in programming, I was able to give Niah a sense of today's modern technologies guiding the future. When I discovered how innately driven to adventure Wish was, I then needed to figure out how her genetic doppelgänger satisfied that craving when trapped in a bubble on a dead world, so the VR element came in and it seemed to be another fascinating twist that made my version of the original Shadow of Nar story unique. After all, video games and VR is another fascination of mine.

Everything seemed to click together and this story became something more than I ever imagined it might be. It's one of those transition books that show an author their potential as an artist, a creator, and also as a businessperson. I hope you've loved reading the story as much as I loved writing it.

There will be at least one more book featuring

Niah and Wish because Niah's health issue is still paramount in the girls' minds. I don't yet know the solution because there isn't one for the real medical condition I gave Niah, so I'll need to reach into science fiction medicine to figure out how that story will unfold. But I'm looking forward to delving into that next adventure in November 2018.

Meanwhile, I'm getting back into the Blood of the Nagaran series, which also involves some genetic components but is a lot more about the mental and emotional battle between what is humane and what is monstrous. It involves people who turn into snakes as well as a hierarchy of angels, an underground cult, and is several dozen shades darker than City of Light.

I hope you'll join me in the stories I still have to tell. If you'd like to know more about those, or get notifications when I have a new book available, you can join the Nagaran by subscribing on my website: rebeccalaffarsmith.com

I also LOVE to hear from readers so feel free to contact me through any of the channels available on my author website. And last but definitely not least, I appreciate to the millionth degree your reviews so please consider taking a couple of minutes right now to share what you loved or hated or want to see more of in a review on your favourite eBook retailer or book review sites.

Yours in the light, and the shadows,
Rebecca Laffar-Smith

Glossary

Transports

Elixr-class IRV: a large Interstellar Research Vessel suitable for between twenty to forty crew and capable of long-range, sustained travel with jump drive.

Settlement Transport: a small hover ship shaped like an Elixr-class IRV but designed to travel between settlements on Nar.

Zip-Glider: a small car-like jet propelled craft that seats four Narians capable of both land-based and space-based transportation.

Launch Wing: a curved wing craft suitable for two-man short distance space or sky flight.

Mini-Zip: a motorbike styled hover craft suitable for swift travel over land.

Zip-Liner: a monorail train using magnetic hover railing

Ocean Liner: a large, cumbersome water-bound ship used for large passenger transfer between landmasses on the surface of Nar.

Measures

Furlong: 250 metres (820 feet); four furlong = 1km (0.62 miles)

Klick: four furlong (1km or 0.62 miles)

Technology

Blaze-cutter: A plasma blow torch.

Plasma Pulser: a laser gun with white-blue pulses of plasma energy that burn searing hot with a kinetic puncture that burns through the flesh of a living being (and can be fatal) but is also highly affective against metal and electronics.

Orkrane: a rare element found in metallic ore on Nar that currently doesn't exist in our periodic table

Sentient: a droid with A.I. designed to mimic Narian life.

Sierra Stars: LED-lit star-shaped hover tech. They can be tossed or suspended in the air to emit a half-furlong of light for several factors per charge.

Solars: the twin stars that Nar orbits

Staple: rations/food - and the true currency of Nar since Shadowfall

Time

Narcycle: a year as measured by one orbit of Nar around its twin solars (15 orbits).

Orbit: a month as measured by one orbit of Nar's third moon around Nar (21 circuits).

Circuit: a day as measured by one revolution of Nar around it's axis (24 factors).

Factor: an hour (60 deccas)

Decca: a minute (60 ticks)

Tick: a second of time.

Lifeforms

Narian: a humanoid born on Nar.

Mamot: a large, lumbering beast of burden a bit like a mammoth but with thick leathery black hide, a narrow mane, a spine down its back, spikes on its tail, large clawed feet, and long tusks above a dog-like snout.

Eagrim: a bird-like creature that is a cross between an eagle and monkey (monkey face - no beak!, eagle body / wings / feet / tail)

Compy/Compathus: a small dinosaur / lizard-like creature very similar to compsognathus with reptilian scales, feathers on its head, a long snout, long tail, muscled hind legs, and small fore legs.

Tiolf: a creature that is a cross between a tiger and a wolf, with fine markings and colourings, soft fur, twin tails, large ears, and large paws. Usually very difficult to tame but can be loyal companions and swift mounts.

Baull: a cross between a bull and a bat, with a stubby body and long thin tail with furry tip, thick hide, twin hoofs on each foot, long bat-like ears, dark-blind eyes, and a flat face.

Chortessa: a large, hideous beast that's a cross between a mutant rat and a werewolf, with large antlers and teeth (plus fangs), claws, a skinny tail, wild eyes, pointed ears, and thick skin with a shag of hair down its back.

Acknowledgements

The creation of a book is never the job of a single person. While I sat and wrote the words, City of Light would never have existed without the contributions of some amazing people, many of them fellow writer friends or readers.

My first thanks goes to **Christine Royse Niles**, **Sean Platt**, and the Smarter Artist Community. Sean created the original outline of Shadows of Nar and Christine convinced him to allow a contingent of Smarter Artists to write their own versions of his story for **NaNoWriMo 2017**. The fellow Smarter Artists who took up the challenge helped problem solve some aspects of the outline and kept me motivated. Without their inspiration and generosity, and the challenge itself, this book would never have existed.

Next up, I must thank my mother, **Stephanie**, and my daughter, **Kaylie**. These two are always my first readers and my proudest supporters. Stephanie offers the non-writer but avid reader perspective and the second dyslexic eye to help smooth out the writing and plot. Kaylie is my brainstorm collaborator. We can talk story and character for hours, and frequently do! Without these two fabulous women my world would be a darker place with significantly fewer words.

I also want to give very special thanks to my wonderful beta readers:

To **Alex Lubansky**, whose detailed notes and insights helped me develop not only the story and characters of City of Light but also the story of the world and, potentially, some other stories within it. Alex gave me technical perspective, sometimes in such detail that it went straight over my head and I had to take the time to unravel and understand it. (Particularly the math!) But I wanted those details, because I wanted City of Light to be true sci fi with minimal wand waving. I wanted it to hold up to real world science as best it could. Alex helped to keep me honest to the laws of the universe as we know them. I still took a little creative license, but any untruths or far-fetched concepts remaining are my own and stem from wilful creative stubbornness rather than ignorance.

To **Jeanne Theunissen**, whose careful eye caught my issues with present tense, my frequently recurring it's/its and lay/lie mistakes among others, and who put in more commas than she took out. There are some comma suggestions I ignored but not because I didn't appreciate the correction of my grammar. The failings of grammar remaining are my own.

To **Rebekah Prince**, who showed me that I could add more layers to the story I had. She helped me see that I hadn't reached the emotional depths this story deserved and that it was worth the time to dig a little deeper into other aspects of the characters' relationships and lives. She was my non-sci-fi reader who, like Jeanne, has an excellent eye for grammar but also looked closely to flow, repetition, and the number of times my characters all bite their lips (all my characters do it in my first drafts, usually because in the moment when they do it as I'm writing, I am doing it myself. ;-))

To **Nanci Nott** and **Chris Milliken**, eager readers both, and personal fans whose own creative ideas and concepts remind me of my joy in writing stories. Your feedback both delights and inspires me. It helped me see some vital flaws in the story, but also the parts where readers resonate with the fun of it all. You're the kind of readers a writer most hopes to reach, eager, engaged, and invested in the story.

Another special thanks goes to my wonderful **Novel Nights Mastermind**. The accountability, inspiration, encouragement, and joviality of the group helped me get through not just NaNoWriMo but also the months that followed as I finished and polished City of Light. I love hearing your vastly ranged concepts and evolving stories and enjoy being part of your journey toward publication and beyond!

My final thanks always goes to **you**, my readers. I hope City of Light has brought you at least a few hours escape from reality and stepped you into an experience of ultimate possibility. I write to unleash the potential of our hearts and minds and I hope, when you put down my books, you're left inspired to live into the greatest version of yourself.

Thank you for reading!

www.ingramcontent.com/pod-product-compliance
Lightning Source LLC
Chambersburg PA
CBHW030631110726
47901CB00002B/404